KU-259-790

THAT'S AMORE

Anna Dunlop's unexciting life takes an upturn when she joins a lively Italian language class. Until her old flame Dante Buonarotti turns up: handsome, charming, confident . . . and a man she still hasn't forgiven for what happened in their youth. When the class takes a trip to Rome, Anna finds herself struggling with her reignited feelings for Dante. In the headily romantic atmosphere of the Eternal City, will the pair finally mend the rift that occurred between them so long ago?

FRANCESCA CAPALDI

◆

THAT'S AMORE

Complete and Unabridged

LINFORD
Leicester

First published in Great Britain in 2019

First Linford Edition
published 2021

A catalogue record for this book is available
from the British Library.

ISBN 978–1–4448–4769–7

Published by
Ulverscroft Limited
Anstey, Leicestershire

Printed and bound in Great Britain by
TJ Books Ltd., Padstow, Cornwall

This book is printed on acid-free paper

Class Act

Anna Dunlop launched herself through her bedroom door, throwing off her grey jacket and struggling out of her skirt as she hopped over the thick pile of the carpet.

'Quick, quick, quick,' she cried, dragging open her wardrobe doors and searching among the items. Perhaps she should have gone straight to the community centre after the long staff meeting, but she wanted to change out of the drab work clothes.

She glanced at the clock, tutting. Discovering the Italian class last September had fulfilled a long-held ambition. She always tried to be there early for it. For that matter, she hated being late for anything.

'Yes!' At last she found the sleeveless yellow dress with the crossover bodice and full skirt. It had been a favourite last summer. It was still only February but today's warm weather had made it feel

1

like early May.

Anna pulled her hair into a pony-tail. Throwing on a white cardigan, she picked up her bag and took the stairs two at a time, slamming the front door behind her.

'I can just make it,' she gasped out, checking her mobile.

She bolted down the dark street. Her work colleague, Dee, was convinced there must be a man involved for her to be this eager. If only.

It had become harder over the years to meet men. The ones she'd dated most recently had been decent enough, but somehow lacking that certain — something.

'What on earth do you want, Annie?' her father always asked after the usual cross-examination about her boyfriend status, or lack of it.

That was part of her problem. What was she looking for? She only knew that it wasn't what was on offer. She'd accepted now that she might never find it.

2

Finally reaching the community centre and flying through the door of the classroom, Anna was dismayed to find someone in her usual seat in the back row, in front of the window. People tended to have an unspoken agreement about where they sat.

Vaguely regarding him, she was aware only that it was a young man. Well, at least that might add interest. The few men who attended were pensioners, nice fellows, but more like her father.

'Signora Dolci, I'm so sorry I'm . . . '

'Come, sit down the front. Ah, but first let me introduce you to our newest student.'

She indicated the young man who stood while the signora spoke, his stiff, straight back emphasising his height. As Anna looked over at him, something in her brain clicked, making her light-headed. She stared at the man but couldn't quite fathom the reason for her confusion.

'Anna, this is Dante Buonarotti. He is half Italian and wants to get in touch

3

with his roots.'

Dante Buonarotti.

Of course it was. It was him being out of time, out of context, that had confounded her. Dante Buonarotti here, of all places.

'Hi, Anna,' Dante said, lifting his hand in greeting, his voice flat. He sat back down.

She lifted her own hand in a mirror action.

'Hello there.'

There was no sign of recognition in his eyes, not a scrap. She made her way to the front row.

'Verbs, the imperfect tense,' Signora Dolci announced, lifting the pen with a flourish as she scribbled several words on the white board.

Dante Buonarotti was behind Anna but on the other end of the row. She faced forward, listening to the tutor's words, her eyes swivelling briefly in his direction every minute or so. Soon she realised she hadn't caught half of what the signora had said.

That was bad. She was the most hard. working student, always did the home-work, and more. Old Terry called her a swot, teasing her in an affectionate way.

What was Dante even doing here? He'd been brought up speaking the language, hadn't he? And what was he wearing? A hand-made designer suit for an evening class? She'd seen enough of them walk into her father's place of work, during holiday employment as a teenager, to recognise quality when she saw it.

After Signora Dolci finished writing up the information, she faced the students.

'Two minutes to learn, then I test you.'

The test was to continue the sentence she gave them with the correct form of the verb. Anna peered at the board as the tutor rubbed off the writing. Signora Dolci picked on the first row, running rapidly along the people there. Unlike her, they'd been paying attention.

'Anna. Your sentence is 'Dante came to the Italian class this evening'.'

Why had she used him in her example?

5

Came. He came. Think, come on, you know this.

'*Dante venive al cla* —'

'No, no, no. Anyone?'

'*Veniva,*' a deep voice called from the back row. '*Dante veniva al classe italiano questa sera.*'

'*Bene, Signor Buonarotti, bene.* Not as rusty as you thought, eh?'

'Guess not.' He looked sheepish.

The tutor moved on to the second row and Anna's chance to impress was gone. Finally the signora returned once again to Dante, giving him several sentences to complete. His answers were perfect. The other students warmed to him, giving little rounds of applause at his successes.

Anna might have warmed to him, too, had she not known him in a former life. She liked to think she wouldn't have been taken in by his act, or by that handsome face and lean bronzed body. Wrong. He would have been as appealing had she met him for the first time tonight as he was all those years ago. And that face that radiated warmth as well as good looks, with the well practised smiles for every occasion. She'd been taken in by it all for seven years straight. But not any more.

Half way through the evening Signora Dolci called a break. The students filed out, creating a hum of chit-chat as they made their way to the canteen. Dante was discussing something with the tutor, charming her with that crooked grin of his. Anna made a beeline for Terry.

'Are you feeling better after last week, Terry? Was it flu?'

'No, I've had my jab. It was just a bit of a cold. Fit as a fiddle I am now.'

They made small talk as they followed the other students. When they reached the small canteen there were three tables left. Terry sat at one, sighing as he heaved his body down.

'The usual?' Anna asked.

'Lovely. You're immensely kind to an old codger.'

'Behave, will you! Bourbon biscuit?'

'You know my little peccadilloes. Two please, if there are enough.'

Anna joined the queue, standing

behind two of the middle-aged ladies, Caroline and Jenny. They were polar opposite in looks. Caroline had a black bob and wore fitted dresses while blonde Jenny, with her long hair, favoured flowing, hippy clothing.

'Nice view,' Caroline said, giving a little giggle as she nudged Anna.

'What is?' Anna said.

'She means our new friend.' Jenny pointed towards where Dante had entered the canteen, still chatting with the tutor.

Anna shifted her gaze swiftly back to the two ladies.

'If you like that kind of thing.'

'Ooh, I do,' Caroline said. 'As they say, if I were twenty years younger . . . ' She sang the first two lines of 'That's Amore' softly, palm flat against her heart. 'Guess you're too young to know that song by Dean Martin.'

There was a pause while Anna composed herself.

'I do know it. My mother has it — had it — on an old LP of his hits. She . . . she loved his songs.' It had been years since she'd heard that album. She didn't even know if her father still had it.

Caroline and Jenny exchanged glances, maybe guessing that something had distressed her.

'Anyway,' Caroline carried on, 'Dante's not your type, then?'

'No. Not my type.' She could have gone into a lengthy explanation for the reason.

Returning to the table with two cups of tea and a couple of the requested biscuits, Anna was dismayed to find Dante seated there, legs stretched out as he leaned back, chatting with the older man.

'Ah, here she is,' Terry said. 'Our other youngster.'

Dante's attention focused on a spot behind her.

'Signora Dolci, thank you so much.' He sprang forward, relieving her of the mug she held out to him.

Unbelievable! He'd already got the tutor waiting on him. He sat back next to Terry, the signora seating herself opposite him. That meant Anna had to sit on the other seat, next to him at the square table.

'Is nice to have a youthful presence in the class,' the tutor said.

Terry grinned.

'Keeps us young.'

Dante looked over to Anna, raising his brow subtly, clearly for her benefit alone. She didn't react.

I shall be old before my time if he comes every week, she thought. She'd found a hobby she really enjoyed and he had to show up to spoil it.

'So, Anna, what do you do?'

It was an odd question now she thought about it. People were usually referring to work, but it could mean anything, couldn't it? What do you do? I sit at home alone most evenings, fantasising about the perfect man, eating my dinner on a tray in front of the history programmes on TV, or with a text book. Pathetic.

'I'm a history teacher. Head of history, in fact,' she said. Not exciting, but

10

respectable, and she did love it.

'Which school?'

Oh dear.

'Telmstone Academy.'

He half smiled, before taking a sip of his drink. It was the school they'd attended, only it had been called Telmstone Comprehensive in those days. Had he remembered her after all?

'What about you?' Terry asked. 'That's a nice bit of cloth you're wearing there. Bet it cost a pretty penny.' Trust Terry to be so candid.

'I have a structural engineering company. We do the building calculations and drawings for high spec buildings.'

'It's good to hear of youngsters making their mark on the world.' Terry nodded to show he was impressed.

Making his mark? His father had owned the same business. He was more likely just following in his footsteps.

Signora Dolci pointed to Anna's dress.

'What a lovely frock you are wearing, my dear.'

'Thank you, signora.'

'Come, Terenzio, there's a poster out here you might be interested in.'

Terry jumped awkwardly to his feet, walking round the table to help the tutor up, even though she didn't need it. As they disappeared through the door, Dante gave Anna the once over.

There was a long, awkward silence, until Dante spoke.

'The signora's right. It's a charming dress. Reminiscent of the Fifties — milk bars, teddy boys and Doris Day.'

The condescending . . .

'How kind of you to say,' she replied, frowning. 'It's nice to change into something more cheerful after being in work clothes all day.'

'Actually, it was a compliment, you know.' He looked down at his own clothes. 'Some of us don't have time to change before leaving work.'

'Because you're so busy with your big company, I suppose.'

He narrowed his eyes, as if not sure how to take her last comment.

'I think I'll go back to the classroom.'

She scraped the chair back, lifting her handbag
off the floor.

'Is it something I said?'

'We only normally get quarter of an hour. I'll go and see what's happened to the signora.'

'Relax, she'll call us when it's time.' He leaned back in his chair. 'I think I'm going to enjoy these lessons.'

'Why have you . . . ?' She stopped herself voicing the question that would make it obvious she knew him.

'What?'

'Why have you joined half way through a term? You must have had to pay for the whole of it. You could have waited till April.'

'When I have an idea I like to act on it straight away, take the bull by the horns, carpe diem and all . . . '

'I get the idea. See you in the classroom.'

'OK — Annie,' he called when she was almost at the door.

Dante watched Anna as she flounced through the dining-room doors. Yes, flounced, like a diva in an over-blown opera. She'd remembered him all right. If he'd had any doubt before, that look after he used her old nickname put paid to it. Had she been like that at school? It wasn't how he remembered her. She'd been quiet, shy. Sweet.

That had been the attraction. She wasn't like some of the other girls, loud and into themselves in a big way. He guessed they'd both changed.

How long had it been since he'd seen her last? Sixteen years? He recalled the painful awkwardness of that morning after the disastrous evening.

She'd continued to be cool with him the whole of that summer holiday after leaving school, out with the gang. Then she'd gone off to uni. He'd thought it a shame at the time, wondered whether he should contact her, put things right. Thank heaven he hadn't if that's what she'd become.

14

Good-looking, though, he couldn't deny that. He'd always liked her shining hair and her skin still had that creamy smooth flawlessness. Not up to the sophisticated standard of his recent girlfriends, but her more natural appearance made rather a refreshing change.

Signora Dolci reappeared, coming half.way into the room.

'Time to go back to the lesson,' she called.

Dante stopped in the corridor, holding the door open for everyone else. There were choruses of 'Thank you, young man,' and 'How polite,' from the more mature students. Jenny and Caroline both winked at him. He was good with names, and could recall almost all of them as they filed through.

The last lady through the door was Ellen, a late octogenarian, at a guess. She walked with a stick, shuffling along slowly.

'Now young man, you may accompany me back,' she said, holding out her arm for him to take.

Anna's eyes strayed to the classroom door each time it opened to admit another student. Nearly all the students were in, but Dante hadn't arrived. Perhaps he'd decided it wasn't for him after all and had left.

It wasn't to be. He strolled in, leading Ellen along while she talked twenty to the dozen, thumping her stick on the ground to emphasise her words.

'He's such a charmer,' she told the class as Dante helped her to her chair, not letting her arm go until she was seated. 'Thank you, you're very kind.'

'You're welcome,' he said, bowing ever so slightly.

A little bit of Anna wanted to like him. Anyone else being so thoughtful would have endeared themselves to her.

As the students put their chairs on the tables at the end of the evening, Dante considered how much he'd enjoyed himself.

When he'd first entered the classroom and seen the ancient participants sitting there, he'd almost done a runner back to his flat, to the lavish sound system and a bottle of Chateau Lafite. He was glad he'd stuck it out. It had been fun — except for Anna Dunlop giving him those moody glares.

Her presence reminded him of that night long ago. No, better to remain firmly in the present, not dwell on the past. Besides, it had made him what he was today. He should be thankful for that.

'I hope you found that useful,' the tutor said, approaching him as he put up the rest of the chairs.

'It's just what I need, Signora Dolci, thank you,' Dante replied.

'We haven't scared you away, then?'

'Certainly not.' Not even Miss Frosty, he added to himself. 'I'll be back next week. And I'll do the homework.'

'Till next week then, Signor Buonarotti.'

En route to the main entrance, Dante buttoned his coat. Ahead, Anna was huddled just inside the door, doing up her cardigan.

'Afraid to go out in the dark?' he asked,

in what he hoped was a joking tone.

She gave him a withering glare.

'I'm waiting for the rain to stop, actually.'

'You'll wait a long time. The weather forecast said it was due to last till tomorrow morning.'

'Oh, no.' She exhaled impatiently.

'Just run for it. Your car can't be too far, can it?'

'I walked.'

'Walked?'

'Yes, you know, that thing you do with your legs.' She raised her eyes heavenward. 'The sky was clear when I left. It's been sunny all day.' She turned sideways on from him.

'It's only the end of February, what did you expect?'

She didn't respond. Other women in her position would have flirted with him, hoping for a lift home.

'I'm curious,' he went on after a moment's hesitation. 'Why didn't you mention we'd met when the tutor introduced us?'

18

'Why didn't you?' She didn't look at him directly. 'Anyway, it would have complicated things, people wanting to know where we'd met, dragging up school days, talking about things long forgotten.'

'Forgotten?' he said, giving a breathy laugh.

She glared at him.

'What's that supposed to mean?'

'Look, if you want to pretend we've never known each other, fine,' he said. 'I'm always pleasant to people I've just met.' Silence. In for a penny . . . 'May I give you a lift home?'

'No, thank you, I wouldn't want to put you out.'

'You're not putting me out.'

'I like walking in the rain. It's very refreshing.'

He unbuttoned his coat, slipping it off his arms swiftly. Leaning towards her, he tried to wrap it round her shoulders.

'Here . . . '

'What are you doing?' She took two steps backwards.

19

'Trying to lend you my coat. What did you think I was trying to do? Kiss you?'

'I most certainly did not!'

'Come on, at least borrow the coat. You'll get soaked.'

'No, I'm fine.' She pushed the glass door outward and stepped into the downpour. She was soon walking briskly away.

'Suit yourself.' Dante struggled to put his coat back on as he caught the swinging door and ran through. He went in the opposite direction from Anna.

Some Things Never Change

On Sunday morning, Anna decided to start on the Italian homework set by Signora Dolci. She wondered if Dante would bother doing it at all. He'd always left things to the last minute at school, though still obtained 'A' grades, much to the exasperation of his friends.

She fetched the notebook out of the bag she'd taken to last week's lesson and looked over the exercise: Using the imperfect tense in a piece about something exciting that had happened to her in the past.

What exciting things had happened to her? Dante asking her out. She could still recall the thrill of him singling her out on the very last day of school. The way he'd smiled, kind of coyly. He'd tucked his hands into his back pockets, leaning against the wall of the sixth form common room. Most people had gone to join the lunch queue, but he'd asked her if he could have a word.

'What is it, Dan?' she'd said when he hadn't been forthcoming.

'Are you looking forward to going out with the gang on Saturday to celebrate?'

'Yeah. No more school. I can hardly believe it.'

There was silence for a few seconds.

'Then what . . . ?' from her and 'I was wondering,' from him came out at exactly the same moment. They giggled.

'You first,' she said.

'What are you doing this evening?' he blurted out, looking at his feet.

'Nothing in particular.'

'Would you like to do something — with me?'

'Oh. Yeah. What did you have in mind?'

He'd taken his hands from his pockets and pushed himself forward, looking her full in the face for the first time.

'A meal at the French place down by the pier?'

'The French place?' She was stalling. He surely wasn't asking her on a date. She didn't want to make a fool of herself.

'The Happy Escargot. You know it?'

'I do. Just the two of us?'

He shrugged.

'If that's OK?'

It was more than OK!

'It's better than sitting at home,' she said casually. 'What time?'

'How about we meet at the pier entrance at seven?'

'Cool.'

Finding their friends, they'd sat at opposite ends of the dining table. No-one would have guessed they'd just agreed to go out. And that had been that.

Anna stared at the empty sheet in her notebook. It had been a long time since she'd gone over that whole conversation. Maybe it wasn't exactly as it had happened, but it was pretty close.

Not that she could possibly use it for her homework. Even if Dante hadn't shown up at the class, this 'amazing' happening in her life had been followed by an equally black one she didn't want to dwell on.

And of course it wasn't the only exciting thing to have happened. Then what to write about? Her first actual boyfriend? She could barely remember what he looked like now. The promotion to Head of History? No, too show-offy.

Rome. The time her mother took her there, as a thirteen-year-old. How she'd loved the relics and the history that Mum had revelled in. She'd longed to go back ever since. Mum had booked a trip for them both, three years ago this coming summer. But then her cancer had returned and it wasn't many months before she passed away.

Anna could have booked a holiday there herself, and had nearly done so on three occasions, but always decided that it was too sad going without Mum. At least she'd be going again soon with some of the Italian group. That was something to look forward to.

She wrote at the top of the page, Una Vacanza a Roma con mia Madre and then the ideas flowed, even if the Italian translation didn't come quite as quickly.

As she was coming to the end, she

looked at the clock. Nearly lunch time. It had taken her two hours. Her dad had asked her to have lunch with him today. She finished the last two sentences and packed the books away.

★　★　★

'Hi, Dad, thought I'd find you round here.' Anna opened the gate and let herself into the back garden.

'Hello, Anna.' Her father straightened up from where he'd been bending over the soil. 'Just getting some weeds out, ready to sow the beans and peas.'

Anna looked round at the neatly dug borders, the abundant blooms of the snowdrops and crocuses and the budding heads of daffodils. 'You've been doing a lot of work out here.'

'I like to keep occupied since I retired, especially outdoors. It's something I didn't get much chance to do when I was working. More's the pity.' He turned away from her, leaning over to cough, his hand covering his mouth.

'I know, but don't overdo it. It does look good, though,' Anna said when he'd recovered and was upright once more.

'Your mum loved the spring flowers.'

'She did.' Anna's eyes became moist. Composing herself after a few seconds, she smiled. 'I'll give you a hand after lunch.'

'Thanks, that'd be much appreciated. I've made lasagne.'

'What, from scratch?'

'Don't sound surprised. Been meaning to give it a try for ages. Your mum taught me how to make it, you know, in the last months. I think she was afraid I'd waste away without her here to feed me.'

Lasagne. Appropriate, given she'd just finished her Italian homework. Her mother had loved cooking Italian food.

'You go and clean yourself up and I'll get the plates out,' she said to her dad.

'You're a love.'

★ ★ ★

26

Dante had had all week to do the homework, yet he'd left it to the day before. He'd been the same at school but had always come away with a good mark.

Things had changed when he'd gone into the business at eighteen and done the structural engineering degree at the same time. No last-minute rushes then.

If he could get the homework done before he left the office he'd be able to relax when he returned home. He didn't have an Italian dictionary here. Never mind, he'd fill in anything he needed to when he got back to the apartment.

There was a brief knock at the door before his personal assistant peeped round.

'You still here, Rachel?' Dante loosened his tie, his fountain pen poised above a sheet of paper.

She pushed the door wider and stepped inside, striking a pose with one leg in front of the other, the knee slightly bent.

'Just finishing getting up to date with the filing.'

'Isn't that what I pay Sarah for?'

'I know, but I like to check it's all done to my specification. You know what a perfectionist I am.' He could have sworn she fluttered her eyelashes, but maybe she had something in her eye.

'And that's what I pay you for,' he said, smiling.

'Indeed. So it's very remiss of me that I forgot to tell you that Ross Harper popped in while you were in the lunchtime meeting.'

'That's a shame, I wanted a word with him. He didn't say what it was about?'

'No.'

'I'll ring him at home.'

'Working late tonight?'

'Just finished. I'm doing — something else, that's all.'

'New client?'

'Um, not exactly. I've, um, started Italian lessons, you know, brush up the language, now we're getting a few clients in Italy.'

'Really? Is your tutor coming tonight, then?'

'No. I'm going to a class at Telmstone

Community Centre.'

'What, with other professionals?'

'One or two,' he laughed. 'But mostly pensioners.'

'You're joking!'

'No, I'm serious.'

'Right.' Rachel strode to his desk, looking down on him. 'Now, I have a friend who runs a company providing private tutors for all sorts of things, including languages. I'm sure he'd be able to find you one.'

For a split second Dante was tempted to take up her offer but then realised he didn't want to leave the class. He didn't want to analyse why.

'Thanks for the offer,' he heard himself saying, 'but you know what? I rather enjoy mingling with the older students.' He added softly and unguardedly, 'They remind me of my own grandparents. Anyway, Signora Dolci seems like a very good tutor. Apparently she used to teach at the Italian Cultural Institute in London.'

'Well, as long as you're happy,' she said, challenging his own resolve.

'I am.'

'When do you do these lessons?'

'Wednesday evening. Doing the homework a bit last minute.'

'I'll leave you to it. Goodnight, Dan.'

'Goodnight, Rachel. See you tomorrow.'

He waited until she'd closed the door before he returned to the sheet of paper in front of him. Something exciting that had happened to him in the past. Mmm.

He could think of plenty of the opposite — his father, the hard grind of building up a business. That was a point. Hard grind it might have been but what a buzz as the projects had been won.

One of his latest had been the redevelopment of the run-down Lido east of the marina — luxury apartments, an opulent theatre, restaurants. It was more impressive than many of the jobs he'd done in London. And now the enquiries were coming in from abroad, notably Italy. No doubt his Italian name was partly responsible for that.

The thrill of building up the business, that's what he'd write about.

★ ★ ★

Anna opened the door to the classroom and peered round. Yes! She made a fist of victory. She was here before Dante.

As she made for her usual seat at the back, she saw Signora Dolci straighten up from her large carpet bag.

'Ah, Anna, even keener than usual. Couldn't be that you're eager to see our latest student, eh?'

'Just mistimed it a bit, that's all.'

Terry came in a few minutes later, accompanying Ellen, followed shortly by Caroline and Jenny, who were giggling.

'Just seen the class hunk,' Jenny said. 'Parking a bea-u-tiful classic Ferrari. She winked at Anna. 'I wonder what's brought him back?'

Anna didn't reply. More students wandered in, chatting, Dante amongst them. He headed to the seat he'd had the week before, stopping dead when he saw Anna sitting there.

'Everyone else is sitting in the same seats as last week.' He undid the zip of an expensive looking leather jacket. At least he'd loosened up a bit this week. She regarded his outfit which included a check shirt and fitted jeans.

'And this is the seat I've sat in every week until you showed up.'

'Ah.'

'Dante, why don't you take this chair at the front?' the tutor suggested.

'Yes,' Anna muttered as he set off to the suggested seat. 'The front's the best place for show-offs.'

'I heard that,' he said.

'You were meant to.'

Signora Dolci looked at her questioningly. Anna shrugged.

'By the way, most people call me Dan,' he said as he made his way to the front.

'You won't mind if I continue calling you by your Italian name?' Signora Dolci said. 'I normally Italianise everybody's name.'

He shrugged.

'I don't mind.'

Just as well, Anna thought. Because I'm not calling him Dan either.

★ ★ ★

'Another victory, Dan m'lad.' Terry rose to take the mid-evening break. 'Yours was definitely the best piece this evening.'

'Thank you, Terry.' Dante bowed his head slightly.

Anna raised her eyes to the ceiling.

'It's great to hear a young man talk passionately about his job. I can tell you're a hard worker,' Terry said.

'It makes it all the more worthwhile when you've done it yourself, built something up from scratch.'

'Quite right, lad, quite right.'

Anna opened her mouth in shock. From scratch! The business had been his father's. He'd been the one to build it up from scratch. What a total fibber the man was.

'You OK, love?' Terry asked. 'Miles away, you look.'

'Pardon? Oh, yes. Just thinking.' Anna straightened her writing book and pen so they lined up.

'Pondering the man of your dreams?'

Dante said.

She narrowed her eyes and stared straight into his.

'Quite the opposite.'

'What's the opposite of pondering the man of your — oh. Thinking about me, by any chance?'

'I never think of you, if I can possibly help it.' She pulled up her bag on to her shoulder, and made for the door.

'Think you started off on the wrong foot with her, m'lad.' Terry grinned.

Dante stared at the door Anna had just walked out of.

'You're right, Terry, I did.'

When they reached the canteen, Anna had already installed herself next to Caroline and Jenny.

'Can I get you a cuppa?' Dante asked Terry.

'Thanks. Milk, two sugars.' He joined Anna's table.

'We're just discussing our trip to Rome,' Caroline said, when Dante returned.

Terry tutted.

'Shame you came to the class a bit late. You could have come too — tenth to the fourteenth of April, it is. It's all booked.'

Anna put her cup down.

'I'm sure Dante has many exotic holidays already planned.'

'As it happens, I don't. I had a lot of work on this year and I haven't got round to booking anything. Shame, that. I love Rome and haven't been there since I was — eighteen.'

The bad bits of that trip came flooding back. He pushed them away, trying to replace them with the agreeable bits — the visits with his mother to places like the Coliseum and the Forum. It would have been good to have another visit there, replace the cruel memories with some more positive ones.

Signora Dolci stood up from the next table and pulled out a chair to join them.

'It may not be too late. We have simply booked flights and a hotel room each. It wasn't any kind of package. There are only us five going.' She indicated round the table. 'It might be worth enquiring.'

Did he really want to go on holiday with this crowd, the flirty middle-aged women, the old timers, the sad young woman?

'OK.'

'Then I'll give you the details before you go home this evening and you can make enquiries.'

He looked over to Anna, about to ask her a question, but she was staring down into her lifted mug, frowning. He'd leave her to it.

* * *

'No, nothing I'm afraid, Dan. I've phoned the airline and the hotel, and they've absolutely nothing.'

Dante was more disappointed than he wanted to let on to Rachel. Maybe it was just as well. He and Anna Dunlop on a holiday together probably wasn't the best idea he'd ever come up with. And he could go to Rome any time he wanted. Then why hadn't he?

'I am not interested, Emily. And I have

36

no money to give you.'

He recalled his father's voice on that fateful trip to Rome, two months after he'd walked out of the house, claiming he was getting clients in Italy. It had all been pie in the sky, and his mother had said so at the time. Antonio Buonarotti simply left his wife and son with a structural engineering business that was going downhill fast, and a house that was mortgaged to the hilt.

After they'd left the Rome apartment, which Dante suspected was owned by a lady friend, his mother had seemed to flick a switch.

'We've five more days here,' she'd said, leading them to a shabby hotel just outside the Termini railway station. 'We will enjoy Rome, see the sights.'

That was the last time his mother had referred to his father until he walked back into their lives briefly four years later, wanting money. By then she and Dante had managed to pull the business out of the mire. With the help of competent staff, and favours from local developer

Ross Harper, they had it ticking over, if not making a huge amount of money. Dante thought at one time that Ross was rather smitten with Mum. Shame it had come to nothing.

Kevin Keen, the father of his one-time friend, Stuart, had harassed his mother with paltry offers to buy her out, not many months after his father had left. But she'd been determined not to give in to his browbeating. This had made the friendship with Stuart strained. Funny that he'd taken over his father's business, too.

Dante pressed the intercom button.

'Rachel, would you look to see what other hotels there are nearby that might have spaces?'

'Already done,' she replied quickly. 'Nothing doing, I'm afraid.'

'Strange. Must be something going on that week. OK. Thanks.'

It wasn't to be.

The Past Catches Up

After Rachel had gone home, Dante stayed on to finish some calculations for a hospital extension they were currently working on.

Having finished the task he idly opened up the internet. Perhaps he'd check some Rome hotels himself, see if there was something, anything. Rachel might only have tried luxury hotels, hung up as she was on him having the best.

He tried half-a-dozen hotels in the vicinity of the one booked by the Italian group, the Sant'Antonio, which was just off the Via Veneto. They all had places. Why on earth had Rachel not managed to come up with anything?

Out of curiosity, he clicked on the Sant'Antonio. There was one room left — a penthouse suite, the only one the hotel possessed. Curious. Instead of trying to book it online, he picked up the phone. This would really give his Italian a workout. Nothing ventured . . .

'Hi, Rachel, you're early this morning.' She jumped as Dante peered round the door between his office and hers, putting the phone down rapidly.

'You got in even earlier than me.'

'I've got plenty to get on with. By the way, I had a look last night, at some hotels. There were plenty of rooms. I even rang the Sant'Antonio and found they had one.'

She frowned.

'Well, I did check on the internet. You know what it's like. These sites don't always have access to all room sales.'

'You could have rung.'

'I don't speak Italian.'

'Maybe you should learn, especially since we're starting to do business with Italy.'

'Maybe I should.'

'Anyway, the receptionist at the Sant'Antonio spoke quite good English.'

'I'll bear that in mind next time. Excuse me, I need to organise some meetings.'

He retreated to his own office. Had she checked at all, or was she trying to stop him hanging out with people she didn't approve of? He decided to give her the benefit of the doubt and believe she was looking out for his best interests.

★ ★ ★

'Nearly all here,' Signora Dolci said as Terry deposited a tray of drinks on one of three round tables they'd dragged together in the pub.

Anna looked round at those from the group who were joining them on their trip.

'There are already five people here. Who else is there to come?'

'Dante.'

'He's managed to get a booking?' The twinge in her stomach made her feel slightly sick.

'Here he is.' Signora Dolci pointed to the door. 'He'll be able to tell you himself.'

'Pint, lad?' Terry asked.

'Half pint, please.'

'OK, we're all here now.' The signora directed Dante to the seat between her and Anna.

'Glad to hear you got a booking, lad.' Terry placed a glass down in front of him.

'It was quite easy. Even managed to get on the same flight.'

'Bene, bene.' Signora Dolci placed a large map of Rome on the table. 'Now, let us decide on an itinerary.'

Anna knew she meant now let's listen to the itinerary I've decided on, but it was all good. She took a notebook and pen out of her bag.

'No need for that, cara, I have handouts.' The signora picked up a bag, pulling out a bundle of stapled sheets.

'Class swot going to take notes?' Dante muttered.

'Looks like you've taken that crown now,' she hissed back.

'Have you something to contribute?' Signora Dolci looked over her glasses from one to the other.

'Just suggesting Anna takes notes of things not on the sheets,' Dante said.

42

'I'm not your secretary,' Anna muttered.

The tutor considered his suggestion.

'That would be a good idea.'

Anna nodded.

'Consider it done, Signora Dolci.'

★   ★   ★

Anna closed her notebook. She'd just finished a list of things necessary to take on the journey. She would type it up and give everyone a copy.

'Thought you weren't a secretary,' Dante said, as she placed the book and pen back in her bag.

'I said I wasn't your secretary.'

'Well, I never,' a new voice announced. 'Annie Dunlop and Dan Buonarotti.'

Anna gasped.

'Stuart Keen. Good heavens. Haven't seen you in years.'

He leaned over to kiss her cheek, then shook hands with an unenthusiastic Dante.

'Seen you from a distance at tender

meetings.'

'Ditto,' Dante said.

Anna noticed the lack of any enthusiasm on Dante's part. Stuart, on the other hand, was beaming at both of them.

'I know Dan's in the structural engineering game like myself, but how about you?'

'I'm Head of History at Telmstone Academy.'

'Our old alma mater. Get you!' Stuart considered Dante. 'I gather you're doing rather well.'

Dante shrugged.

'We get by. I gather you're doing OK, too.'

'Well, you know. Seems like a long time since we were all at school together.'

'You two already knew each other?' Terry pointed from Dante to Anna, gaining the attention of the rest of the group.

Anna cringed. How on earth would they explain not saying anything in the first place? She was about to open her mouth to give some explanation, forming it on the hoof, when Dante got in before her.

'We knew each other at school a long time ago. Neither of us was sure until the end of class, when we walked to the entrance together.'

'What, you thought there might be two Dante Buonarottis in the area?' Caroline indicated Dante with an outstretched hand.

'I realised it must be him,' Anna explained. 'But I wasn't sure if he remembered me. My name isn't out of the ordinary.'

Stuart grinned.

'Who could forget you? Talking of schools, I hear the council's asking for tenders for the old comp up on Roebury Brill. You going for that, Dan?'

'Possibly.'

'You mean Holling Comp?' Terry asked. 'I knew it when it was Holling Secondary Modern, and before that just Holling School. Always having to change things. You take that new complex down past the marina. Nice bit of beach there was before, with what was a grand old lido once upon a time.'

'Ah, now you'll have to talk to Dan about that. I believe it was his company that worked on it.'

'Is that right?' Anna turned to where Dante had tucked himself into a corner.

'Yes,' he confirmed. 'That is, we worked out the technical stuff that stops it falling down.'

'Why'd they do it?' Terry asked.

'The lido wasn't fit for repair. They could have left it to decay further or pulled it down. The third option was to redevelop it. If you'd like to meet for a pint sometime, I'd be happy to explain it in more detail to you, Terry. But now,' Dante looked at his watch, 'I have an appointment I can't afford to miss.'

'On a Saturday, lad?'

'Yep. That's business these days, I'm afraid.' Dante drank down the last half inch of his beer and bid them a general farewell.

'Did I say something to offend him?' Stuart said.

'He seems to be offended by

46

everything.' Anna dismissed him with a wave of her hand. 'Wouldn't take any notice. I don't.'

'You and Buonarotti aren't an item, then?'

'No!' She moved away from the group a little and Stuart followed.

'Just seem to remember you were rather into each other at school.'

Anna looked round to make sure no-one else had heard.

'Not really. And that was a long time ago!'

'I've not seen you in here before.' Stuart peered round the room as though he was searching for someone.

'I haven't been before. We're having a meeting of our Italian class, that's all.' She indicated towards them. They were all looking back, curiosity in their faces.

'And Dan belongs to that? Thought he was Italian.'

'Half. Brushing up on far from fluency was how he put it.'

'And you two kept in touch?'

'No.'

'But . . . '

'Coincidence.' Anna sighed. 'Hadn't seen him in sixteen years.'

'All the girls at school thought he was dead gorgeous.'

Anna sniffed.

'Did they? Bit obvious for me.'

Stuart chuckled.

'Do you fancy a meal out at some point in the future? Catch up on old times?'

'Perhaps.' She wanted to appear interested but not too eager. He was rather handsome, with the chiselled features, neat, fair hair and designer stubble. And he had manners, not like Mr Grumpy. 'Give me a call, and we'll see what we can arrange.'

They exchanged numbers.

'Dante gone?' Terry deposited a tray of drinks on the table for the ladies.

'Yes,' Anna replied. She walked back towards them and Stuart joined her.

'Shame, I was wondering whether he'd heard anything about the rumoured redevelopment of the Community Centre,' Terry said.

'Where we have our lessons?'

'That's right. Lovely Victorian red brick building. That's never past its sell-by date. And what's more, it was left to the people of Telmstone fifty years ago by Sir Mortimer Jenkins. They've no business pulling it down.'

Stuart screwed up his eyes.

'Where'd you hear this?'

'My daughter, Megan. She works in one of the offices up at the council and heard it from someone. You know anything, since you're in the same trade?'

Stuart shook his head slowly.

'I'd better get going. I told my parents I'd pop round to see them.'

'Would you be able to make some enquiries?' Anna said.

'Sure thing.' Stuart walked to the side door. 'I'll ring you,' he said as he left.

'That was a quick meeting!' Terry called, watching as Dante heading back towards them from the front door.

'Forgot my coat.' He picked up the leather jacket from the back of a chair.

'I was just saying to the others, I heard

a rumour the council might be thinking of pulling down the centre where we have our class. Something about a luxury shopping complex.'

Dante regarded him, open-mouthed, for a couple of seconds.

'Nonsense. You shouldn't take notice of idle rumours.'

'I don't know. My daughter said . . .'

'She should be careful what she spreads around.' Dante put the jacket on.

'Stuart didn't seem to think it was idle gossip,' Anna said. 'He seemed concerned.'

'Did he now? Got to dash.'

And he was gone again.

'He didn't seem very happy,' Terry said.

'No.' Got to wonder why, she thought, before tugging her attention back to the general conversation.

Tea for Two

'Can I come in?' Stuart called, waiting at Anna's door while she fetched her bag.

'No point, I'm ready.' She ran back to the hall the best she could, given the height of her heels. 'There, done.' She pulled the shawl from the newel post and closed the door behind her.

'You look nice.'

Mission accomplished! She had on the yellow dress she'd worn the first night Dante had come to class. Stuart clearly appreciated it more than he did.

'Thank you, kind sir. OK, where are we going?'

He took her arm and led her to his car, a red Porsche. Very nice.

'La Giaconda, in Littlebay. You know it?'

'Not at all. I don't have much call to go into Littlebay.'

'You should, there's a great beach there.' He opened the passenger door, inviting her to step inside.

'Could we have a walk along it after?'

'Not in this gear.' He flapped a hand up and down towards himself, indicating the pressed chinos, smart jacket and stylish shirt.

Come to think of it, her heels wouldn't be too good on the sand, but she could have slipped them off, gone barefoot. She hadn't done that in a long while.

'I have to say, you're looking rather dapper yourself.'

'I aim to please.' It was delivered with a rather coy expression. How refreshing after Mr I Am, otherwise known as Dante Buonarotti. Right, no more thoughts about him. She'd been doing that too much recently.

They chatted about old school acquaintances as they drove in the sun in his convertible, roof down, to the village seven miles east of Telmstone. When they arrived, he rushed round to open the car door for her, taking her arm to accompany her through the restaurant entrance.

Anna looked round at the chic décor, the cream tablecloths and slim vases with a single rose each. Classical music played softly in the background. The delicious aroma of tomato and garlic tantalised her taste buds.

'Fancy this being tucked away down here.'

'You wait till you try the food.'

They were soon seated with menus in front of them.

'I could take a month of Sundays to choose,' Anna said. 'Everything sounds amazing.'

'If you want to make it easy, I recommend the scallops and the lobster thermidor. If you're into fish.'

'Perfect.'

Stuart ordered, choosing the wine as well. When the waiter had returned and poured them each a glass, Stuart lifted his to clink it with Anna's.

'Cheers!'

'Cheers. Stuart, you said last Saturday you'd enquire about the Community Centre development.'

He took a sip of the wine.

'Not had an opportunity yet. I'll try to

remember next week.'

'Thank you. It would be a crying shame for anything to happen to that building. It's such a lovely example of Victoriana.'

'Of course. You're a historian.'

'Yes. Therefore I do have a kind of vested interest — quite apart from the fact I go to lessons there. They hold a huge amount of classes.'

'So I gather. If the worst came to the worst, there are other council buildings they could be relocated to.'

A waiter came to the table, depositing a basket of bread. Anna waited until he was out of earshot before she continued.

'But why go to the bother? And that building fits in with the other Victorian houses. But you must realise that yourself, being a structural engineer.'

He was staring past her. Oh dear, was she boring him? She stopped talking and his attention came back to her.

'Sorry, I just saw someone over there I'd rather avoid.'

Anna looked round to see a middle-aged man with a woman she

presumed to be his wife.

'Him or her?'

'Him. Let's just say we had professional differences. But back to what you were saying. Yes, those houses are no doubt splendid. I'm sure there are many who'd consider it fine real estate, too.'

'I'm sure they would.'

'Sorry, I'm talking shop.' He lifted his glass and made a toast. 'To you and the good fortune I had meeting you again.' Anna grinned and lifted her own glass.

* * *

'Look, here it is.' Terry stabbed his finger at a page of the local newspaper, sitting in the canteen at break time.

'Here's what?' Caroline peered over his shoulder.

'What I was talking about, at the pub. The council's going to pull this lovely building down and put up one of those luxury shopping complexes. And in a town with perfectly decent shops!'

'Let me have a look at that.' Dante

took the paper, skimming it with some impatience. 'It only says there are possible plans for development on Grand Parade.'

Anna rose to take a look.

'That's the road we're on.'

'But that doesn't mean they're knocking down this building.' Dante read a bit more of the blurb. 'Nor does it say they're building a shopping complex. Where did you get that from, Terry?'

'That's what my daughter said. And there's no smoke without fire.'

'Trust the paper not to have any sources.' Dante shook his head. 'I'd love to know who wrote that, getting everybody upset.' He might have a word with the editor, see what he could find out.

Terry thumped his fist on the table.

'We must swing into action!'

'We could protest.' Caroline rubbed her hands together. 'Get the rest of the classes involved. Make banners and tie ourselves to the railings.'

'There aren't any railings,' Dante pointed out, wondering how to knock the conversation on the head.

'Spoilsport!'

'*Cari, cari,*' Signora Dolci said. ' Nothing can be achieved in this haphazard way. Now, Dante, this is your line of work. You've heard nothing about any plans for this centre or the street?'

'There's nothing gone out to tender.'

The tutor nodded sagely.

'Well, it seems to me that we need to get our facts right before we do anything.'

'But what if something underhand is going on?' Anna said. 'After all, this is the second time we've heard about it. First Terry's daughter, now the paper.'

Dante had wondered when she was going to have her say. That was all he needed, people poking their noses in, causing problems before he'd managed to sort things out.

'Could be someone just causing trouble.'

'For what purpose?' Anna persisted. 'Either way, like Terry said, there's something going on.'

'By the way, I think tea break ended

five minutes ago. The other classes have gone back.' Hopefully that would bring the discussion to an end.

'This is important!' Anna snapped. 'I would have thought you'd be as concerned as we are.'

'Look, I don't make it a habit of jumping to conclusions, that's all.'

'Dante is right, Anna,' the signora said. 'I think we should ask him to look into it first, before we decide on any action. If that is OK?' The tutor regarded him.

Dante stifled his heavy sigh, letting it out slowly and silently instead.

'I'll make an enquiry.'

* * *

As she was leaving the centre that evening, Anna caught up with Dante in the entrance hall.

'You are going to make enquiries, aren't you?'

'I said I would.'

'I don't know why you're being so hostile about it.'

'Me being hostile? I'll leave that to you would-be protestors who want to chain yourselves to non-existent railings.'

'You were getting pretty cross about us talking about it. Something's not right.'

'Only in that brain of yours.' He tapped the knuckles of one hand against his head.

'Since you've wheedled your way on to our holiday . . . '

'Wheedled?'

'Not to mention managing to secure the position of Signora Dolci's pet . . . '

'Stop it!'

'Then at least you could do that small thing for us. It wouldn't take much of your time, with your contacts.'

'I might just be adding fuel to a fire that doesn't even exist.'

Anna could feel a headache forming.

'You really are the most difficult man!'

'And you're very attractive when you're angry.'

Anna rolled her eyes.

'Don't you take anything seriously?'

'Of course I do, otherwise I wouldn't

have a thriving business. Look, let's start again. How about a drink, then I'll give you that lift home you refused the first night?'

'No, thank you!'

She stormed out, flinging the outer door open but not bothering to hold it there for him.

'Charming!' she heard him call after her as she thundered off.

She was two streets away before she slowed down and looked up. It was amazing how much lighter the evenings had become in the last couple of weeks, though the temperature was no warmer. She shivered and fastened her coat.

Only eight days till Rome. Thoughts of Dante accompanying them made her grimace. Stuart had been eager to help find out what was going on. Why was Dante being cagey? There was something she couldn't quite put her finger on.

As she walked, she let her mind wander to her next date with Stuart. Pity he hadn't been able to make it in the week at all. She was really looking forward to seeing him again. She was pondering this, turning on to her own street, when it occurred to her.

Dante had never once directly answered the question as to whether he knew anything.

★ ★ ★

'Not as elegant as La Giaconda,' Stuart peered out of the window of the tea room, towards the sea, 'but it's good for afternoon tea.'

'I love it. I used to come here with my mum.' Anna breathed in deeply, willing her chin not to wobble. Stuart was looking straight at her and she waited for the question.

'So why don't you and Dan Bounarotti hit it off any more? You got on fine at school.'

Not the question she'd expected, but maybe it was as well to be distracted.

'That was a long time ago, Stuart. He's different. Full of himself. I hardly recognised him when he first stepped into the class.' So not true, though it had taken a while for her confused brain to gather itself into rational thought.

'Guess it goes with the business, the self-assurance.'

'This is arrogance. Quite different. And you're in the same business but you're not like that.'

'I guess I can be like that, too, in business. You have to be.'

Anna leaned forward.

'By the way, did you hear anything about the town redevelopment?'

He lifted the teapot lid and peered inside.

'Do you fancy another pot of tea? I do.'

'Why not?'

Stuart called the waitress over.

'We've been lucky with the weather today,' he said after she'd gone.

'Stuart, don't you start this.'

'What?'

'Avoiding answering direct questions about the rumoured redevelopment. I've had enough of that from Dante.'

'Is that right?' He leaned in, his eyes questioning.

'Yes. I'm beginning to think he's behind it, or at least, has something to do with it.'

'Mmm.' Stuart frowned. 'You think that's a possibility?'

'Then the development isn't just a rumour?' Deep inside she had hoped she was wrong about this.

'Hard to say. But please, keep that to yourself. We don't want people going in, all guns blazing.'

'But those affected have a right to know.'

'Maybe, but I'd like to know how deep Buonarotti's in it first.'

'You mean, do a bit of an investigation? Expose him?' She considered this for a while. 'You know Councillor Stacey's always been a bit . . . iffy. There was that scandal last year, about him getting back-handers from the developers of some luxury flats.'

'Never proven. Might have been the newspapers overreacting to something quite innocent. Harry Fellows, the editor of the 'Telmstone Times', has no love for Councillor Stacey because he went up in an election against him and lost. Like I said, keep quiet for now. Unfounded rumours aren't good.'

'You're right. And despite what he's like, I wouldn't want to get Dante into trouble if he's not involved.'

'Lovely! Here's the tea.'

Another Woman

Dante had purposely kept quiet during the last couple of classes unless he was asked a direct question. He'd proved himself capable for the intermediate class — he could sit back for a bit without feeling like a fraud. He didn't want to annoy the other students by always putting his hand up and getting the answers right. Including Anna.

He was ready for a coffee by the time the break came, taking Ellen by the arm, at her request, leading her along to the canteen, alongside Signora Dolci.

'No Terry tonight?' Ellen said as she limped along. 'You heard from him, signora?'

'I haven't, cara. Which isn't like him.'

'Hope he's OK.'

In the canteen, Dante sat Ellen down whilst he fetched her tea. When he arrived back, Anna had joined the table.

'Have you looked into whether there are any plans for redevelopment here yet?' Anna sat opposite, though she was looking at her mug, not him.

She was like a stuck record.

'I assume you're talking to me,' Dante said irritably.

'Who else?'

He regarded her for a couple of seconds and sighed.

'I can assure you it will all be fine.'

'You can assure me? What, the great Dante Buonarotti can guarantee it?'

'Now, now, cari,' Signori Dolci leaned over them. 'Play nice, eh?'

Dante didn't react to the signora's request, staring intensely at Anna instead.

'I'll do my utmost.'

The door was flung open abruptly and Terry made his way across the canteen.

'Terribly sorry I'm late,' he puffed. 'Was looking after my grandchildren — Megan had a bit of an emergency. Phew! At least I've made it for the second half.'

'Let me get you a drink,' Dante offered.

'Tea'd be great. And a coupla bourbons. Ta, lad.'

When he returned with the order balanced on a tray, Anna was addressing the others.

'Dante assures us there's not going to be a redevelopment here.'

'Not quite what I said . . .'

'Well, funny you should say that.' Terry lifted a local newspaper from the tote bag he kept his Italian books in. 'Says the same thing here, on page five.'

Anna took the paper and opened it.

'Rumours of a new shopping development on and around Grand Parade have no foundation, it was revealed today,' she read.

'Foundation. Oh, ha ha,' Dante said.

'Anyway! It goes on to say, 'Sources close to Councillor Stacey assure us that it is all pie in the sky.' Whatever that means.'

'Wouldn't trust Councillor Stacey,' Terry said.

Anna put the paper down.

'You think it might be a cover-up?'

'Mmm, dunno.' Terry tapped his chin. 'The thing is, the editor of the 'Telmstone Times' has no love for Bill Stacey, so I can only conclude this is true.'

Nice one, Harry, Dante thought. Good bit of double bluff. Just as well he'd got on to him after the first newspaper report.

Anna shook her head.

'That's not what Stuart told me.'

'Stuart?' Dante said. 'When did you see him?'

'Last weekend.'

He noticed her shift awkwardly, then fiddle with her hair.

'Where was this?'

She looked him square in the eyes.

'Not that it's any of your business, but it was while we were having tea on the sea front. And the week before he treated me to dinner at La Gioconda in Littlebay.' The widening of her eyes seemed to add, so there!

Not good. This would make the whole affair more complicated.

'What a fantastic place that is,' Anna continued. 'The food's out of this world.'

'Starting seeing him, have you?'

Anna hesitated.

'We've been out a couple of times, if that's what you mean. I used to know him well. You knew him even better.'

'Yes, but that was years ago. You should be careful with people you don't know well.'

'That'd be a boring existence,' Caroline butted in, leaning over from the next table. 'If we never got to know someone new. We wouldn't have come to this class for a start, or be going off on holiday to Rome together. You go, girl! He was cute.'

Dante picked his mug up.

'Cute!' he mumbled before taking a sip, refusung to admit his feelings of disquiet.

★ ★ ★

Anna unpacked her Italian books and put them in their places on the shelf. She went over the conversation with Dante. Who on earth was he to tell her who she should see? The nerve of the man! Anyone would think he was her father.

Which reminded her, she hadn't rung Dad this week yet. It was after ten, but he'd always been a night owl. She picked up the phone.

'Hi, Dad, how are you?'

'OK. Just about to go to bed.' He sounded strained, breathless.

'That's not like you.'

'No. Feeling a bit tired. What have you been up to?'

'Just got back from the Italian class. Do you remember Dante Buonarotti, from when I was at school?'

'The Italian kid you were friends with? Indeed I do. His mother had the structural engineering company up on the Whitedean estate. My old boss, Ross Harper, used them to do a fair amount of the structural calculations for his developments.'

'Do you mean his father, not mother?' Anna said.

'I don't think so. I remember dealing with Emily Buonarotti first, then later, Dante as well.'

'Anyway, he started at the class a

few weeks back. Hadn't seen him since before I started uni. He's so full of himself it spoils the class a bit.'

'That's a shame.' There was a sigh.

'You don't sound yourself, Dad.'

'I've a bit of indigestion.'

'How about I come over Sunday, make you a meal?' Anna offered. 'You don't feed yourself properly.'

'I do fine, but yes, I'd like to see you. You haven't been over in three weeks.'

'Yes, sorry. Gets a bit busy this time of year at school, working up towards exams.'

'Guess it does. Ooh, excuse me.' There was a pause. 'Sorry about that, can't stop yawning. Better get to bed.'

'OK, Dad. See you Sunday.'

As she replaced the receiver, she remembered Stuart. He hadn't been available during the week so he might want to do something at the weekend. Hopefully Saturday.

Her stomach did a little dance. Early days yet and they hadn't even kissed, but who knew where it would go? After all this time, it would be more than weird to end up with someone from school.

★ ★ ★

Dante pushed open the door between his office and his PA's. She was talking on the phone.

'I've already told you — no!'

Her eyes were wide with the guilt of someone caught doing something they shouldn't be.

'Don't ring me again,' she snarled, before ramming the phone down.

He regarded her questioningly.

'You know I don't mind you making personal phone calls. As long as you don't take the mick and do it all day long.'

'No. Yes. I know. It was just a bit too personal. Sorry.'

'No need to apologise. Ex-boyfriend not leaving you alone again?'

She shrugged.

'OK. I'll mind my own business,' he said. 'But if you need help with some trouble, let me know.'

'Did you want me for something?'

'Yes, please. I had a careless moment and managed to knock over the two piles of calcs for Lyndleys and Dales.'

'Oh dear!'

'Exactly. Calcs pages spread wide and all mixed up. Don't know why they insist on paper copies. Luckily they're numbered and have headers.'

'I'll sort it,' she said. 'You get on with what you need to.'

'Thanks, you're a star. I do need to get some other work done for Ross Harper, which I promised to finish by seven this evening.' That reminded him that he needed to speak to Ross about that other business again.

'Don't worry, I'll stay for as long as it takes.'

By the time Rachel had finished picking up the pages, sorting them into their own piles and reprinting any that had been damaged, Dante had also finished his work.

'Think I'll knock off early tonight.' He shut down his computer as Rachel carried the piles to a filing cabinet and placed them there. 'It is Friday, after all.'

'Everyone else went ages ago. You need more down time,' she said.

'Which is what I'm going to have now. Care to join me? I was thinking of trying a new restaurant — La Giaconda, in Littlebay.'

'Littlebay. How quaint.'

'Meant to serve excellent food, though. Take it as a thank you for all the work you've put in recently. Over and above.'

She smiled, her head bent forward as her eyes lifted shyly to regard him.

'Of course I'll join you. Only had leftovers from last night planned for this evening anyway.'

What a gracious attitude, he thought. Not like Anna Dunlop. They were both attractive, but that's where the similarities ended. Anna did everything to avoid him while Rachel couldn't do enough for him. Pity he didn't feel that certain spark for her.

Rachel, that is. Well, either of them. Rachel was maybe a tad too bossy. But she'd be good company this evening and no harm done. It beat cooking for one and sitting in front of the TV.

★ ★ ★

'This is a bit of a surprise.' Rachel glanced around, taking in the décor of the restaurant.

'Had a glowing report on it, though I had my doubts,' Dante said. 'I'm glad to find it lives up to expectations so far.'

'Who recommended it to you?'

'Oh, one of my Italian class.' Hopefully Rachel would leave it at that.

She looked up from the menu.

'Who was it, then?'

He paused, making it look like he was trying to recall her name.

'Anna. She came here with her boyfriend a while back.' That should allay any suspicions.

They'd almost finished their main course when Dante heard a familiar voice behind him. He turned to see Stuart Keen hanging on to a leggy redhead.

'Hello, Stuart. Fancy seeing you here.' Dante lifted a hand in greeting.

'Oh, hi, Dan. Yeah. Fancy.'

Rachel twisted round suddenly, scowling at Stuart as if he were an unwelcome interruption. He, on the other hand, gave her a smile that said he liked what he saw. Rachel looked away quickly. The woman with him didn't notice, her appreciative stare fixed on Dante.

'Not with Anna tonight?' Dante enquired.

'Anna?' Stuart looked at his partner, who frowned back at him.

'Yes. You brought her here a couple of weeks back, didn't you?'

'Oh, that Anna. Of course. Nice meal with a friend, catching up on old times.'

'Of course. Have a good meal.' It was a dismissal from Dante.

A waiter arrived and escorted Stuart and the young woman to their table.

'You all right?' Dante asked, seeing Rachel's expression. 'You've gone a bit pale.'

'Yes, I'm all right. Um, Stuart Keen,

well, he reminds me of someone I'd rather forget.' She picked up the glass of water and took a long drink.

'He is someone I'd rather forget. We were at school together.'

Rachel placed the glass down slowly, looking puzzled.

'Really? I didn't know that.'

'No reason why you would.'

'The Anna you mentioned, is that the one from your class?' Rachel asked while Dante was still looking at where Stuart had been seated, thankfully on the other side of the room.

'Yes,' Dante replied.

'But he's with someone else and referred to her as a friend.'

'So it would seem.'

'Are you going to tell her?'

'I've no idea. Probably wouldn't be appreciated.' The last comment was more to himself. 'It's made me wonder.'

'What about?' Rachel regarded him. Dante felt a vague discomfort.

'A little investigation . . . Are you available for some overtime?'

She leaned in like a conspirator, her chin resting on the back of her hand.

'What for?'

'I need to figure that out. And please feel free to say no if you don't want to do it.'

'Now I'm really intrigued.'

'Don't get your hopes up for too much excitement . . . Dessert?'

Calling a Truce

Dad? Dad!' Anna had knocked on the door several times to no avail and was now using her spare key to get in. His car was on the drive but he might have walked somewhere.

'Dad?' She opened up the living room door to find him slumped on the sofa, still in his pyjamas. 'Oh my goodness, Dad!'

She rushed over to him as his eyes opened and he looked round, confused.

'What's happened?' he said.

'Are you all right?' She sat next to him, gently easing him to a sitting position.

'Just fell asleep, that's all. Forty winks.'

'At midday?'

'Didn't sleep well last night.'

'What's wrong? You're a bit pale.'

He clutched his stomach.

'Think I might have that virus that's going around, that's all. Might be better if you went home. You don't want to catch something before you go to Rome.'

'Well, no.' She stood up. 'But I don't want to leave you like this, either. I've brought something to make lunch. And have you got food in the house?'

'A bit.'

'I'll go and look, and get you a cup of tea.'

She went to the kitchen and clicked the kettle on, checking her father's food stores as she fetched the milk out of the fridge. There were a couple of carrots, some sliced meat which had gone past its sell by date and a bit of dry cheese. Even the milk was on its date.

Having made the tea, she took it back to her father.

'Your fridge is virtually empty, Dad. What on earth have you been living on?'

'Haven't felt like eating the last couple of days. Haven't shopped since last weekend.'

'Why didn't you ring me?'

'You've enough on your plate with work.'

'Don't be daft. I could easily have got you some things on the way home. Right,

80

I'm going to the shops now. When I get back, I'm cooking you some meals to put in the freezer. That way you can get one out every morning and just let it defrost.'

'You're too good to me. Haven't you got a life?' he said.

Not so you'd notice, she thought.

'Yes, and it includes you. If you're still like this on Wednesday, I'm not going to Rome.'

'You jolly well will,' he said, perking up.

'You've got the opportunity, now grab it. You don't do enough for yourself. I'll be fine.'

★ ★ ★

Anna had rung her father every day the following week. He'd given her the same answer — *I'm much better today*. She wasn't sure if he was spinning her a line, so on Wednesday she decided to call around on her way to Italian, to check he was OK.

He answered the door thirty seconds after she knocked, beaming at her as he beckoned her in.

'Thought you might check up on me. Look, I'm fine and dandy.' He proved it by walking to the kitchen door and back, though was slightly hunched over. 'And I'm dressed.'

'You're still looking a little pale.'

'I'm all right, I tell you. I haven't seen the sun in a few days, that's all.' He emitted a rasping cough.

'Dad!' She took hold of his arm.

When he stopped coughing he took a couple of breaths.

'It's just the end of a cold. Don't fuss. And thank you for the meals.'

'Do you want me to do some more?'

'I've still got some left, and I'm sure I can manage to get my own food now, anyway. Haven't you got an Italian class to get to?'

'I have, but I want to make absolutely sure you're OK before I go. Or I won't go. And as I told you, I'll cancel my trip.'

'And as I said, no you won't. Now, off you go.' He patted her along the hall.

She turned towards him before she

reached the door.

'Anyone would think you were trying to get rid of me.'

'I am. There's a programme I want to see in five minutes, and I'm going to heat some food up first.'

'All right. As long as you're sure.'

'Go!'

'Bye, Dad.' She kissed his cheek before letting herself out.

★ ★ ★

'All ready for tomorrow?' Caroline inspected her orange fingernails as Anna took her seat.

Anna sighed.

'Still have to iron a couple of bits. I wasn't absolutely sure if I'd be going till this evening.'

'You weren't going to Roma? Why is that, cara?' Signora Dolci paused from writing the date in Italian on the board.

'Who isn't going to Rome?' Dante stepped through the door.

'Anna. She didn't know if she would

83

come or not,' Caroline said.

'Scared you off, have I?' Dante looked amused.

'My father's been ill, some kind of virus, apparently.' She told them how she'd found him on Saturday. 'I wanted to make sure he was well before I finally decided. That's all.'

'But he's OK now?' Dante looked genuinely concerned.

'Yes. I called round tonight and he's walking about and has his appetite back.'

'That's good. But surely your mother's there to look after him anyway.'

There was a pause where she felt the familiar longing.

'My mother died two years ago,' she said quietly.

His eyes widened.

'Oh. I'm sorry. I didn't know.'

'Why would you?'

Their attention turned to the signora.

'OK, you're all here. I know you're not all coming to Roma tomorrow, but I thought we'd do a few role plays, practise our tourist Italian. Let's see how you'd manage in *un ristorante.*'

At break, Dante noticed Anna take the last seat on a table with Caroline, Jenny and Terry and he cursed his luck. There was something he was curious about, but it would have to wait till later. He placed Ellen's tea on the table in front of her, sitting to chat to her and the other older folk.

As they got up to leave, Anna gathered up the cups from her table to return to the counter. Dante did the same, waylaying her on the way back to the door. Everyone else had left the canteen.

'Seen anything of your boyfriend recently?' he enquired.

She came to a halt, eyeing him with disdain.

'You mean Stuart?'

'How many boyfriends have you got?'

'Oh, loads. As usual, is it your business?' She tried to get past him but he was standing in the doorway.

'Just curious. I saw him a couple of weeks ago.'

'Where?'

'Just around.'

She waited a few moments, eyebrows raised, as if wanting him to continue. When he didn't she opened the door and entered the corridor in the direction of the classroom. He caught her up, nearly bumping into her as she stopped abruptly.

'I haven't seen him in that time,' she said. 'I don't know what you're implying but he's been away and told me he'd be very busy when he got back. Just what do you mean by around?' Her eyes narrowed, challenging him.

'At some meeting or other.'

'I see. Big deal. We're meeting up after I get back from Italy. Shall I send him your love?'

No reply was forthcoming and she walked off. Either she knew about the redhead and didn't want to lose face or . . . Yes, probably the 'or'.

'Looking forward to tomorrow?' he called after her.

'I was.' She stopped again, to scowl at him. He frowned at her in reply. 'OK,

I am. Despite your presence. Just don't spoil it.' She wagged her finger at him.

'I'll be as good as gold.' He put his hands up in surrender.

'You'd better be.'

* * *

Anna stood on the pavement outside her house at six o'clock the following morning, waiting for Caroline to pick her up. She was still thinking about what Dante had said. Stuart did seem to have cooled off. His promise to see her after she came back from Italy had been a little strained when he'd rung her to cancel a date they'd made.

He'd sounded tired, saying things were complicated and he had a lot of work coming up. He was probably stressed. Never mind, she'd find him a little present in Rome and treat him to a night out when she returned.

At the airport she, Caroline, Jenny and Terry soon found Signora Dolci, along with Dante.

'We'll check in now.' The signora led the way to the desk.

They each lifted their cases on to the conveyor belt. Signora Dolci asked the member of staff there if they could all sit together.

Dante put his expensive leather hold-all up last, handing his ticket to the attendant.

'Except for me.'

The attendant examined his ticket and looked up to say something, but smiled instead, her eyes crinkling round the edges. How predictable, Anna thought. He's going to charm her to get some better position, no doubt.

'Well of course, sir. You'll be seated in business class.'

Terry looked at him in surprise.

'You're in business class, lad?'

'Not by choice.' Dante stepped back to face them all. 'I tried to book economy, but it was full up. Business was all that was left.'

Anna crossed her arms across her chest.

'I bet.'

'It's true. I thought better that than getting a different flight.'

'Fine.' Her mouth puckered and she stared ahead. She should be happy that his annoying presence would be elsewhere, but a tiny bit of her felt slighted.

* * *

'Good flight,' Terry said, as they gathered by the luggage carousel. 'Though I dare say Dante's was even better.'

'It was fine,' Dante said, though he'd missed the company.

Signora Dolci lifted her case down.

'Let us take two taxis to the hotel.'

'You are at the same hotel, I suppose?' Anna said.

'Yes. Yes I am.' That at least was true. She wasn't going to be happy when she found out where exactly.

As the others started wheeling their cases towards the exit, Dante came up beside Anna.

'Look, for the duration of the holiday,

can't we call a truce? Whatever happened when we were younger that's got you riled was a long time ago. Let's keep it there.' 'What makes you think it's got anything to do with that? It's what you're like now — arrogant.'

'It's only you seems to think that. Yeah, I'm self assured, but that's different. If you want arrogant, I'd point the finger at Stuart Keen.'

She twisted towards him, grasping his arm to stop him.

'On what evidence?'

'He just is.'

'Well I'll thank you to keep your opinions to yourself. Stuart's a lovely guy who's very caring.'

'Yes, caring to everybody.'

'What's that supposed to mean?'

He put his hand on her arm.

'Nothing. Look, for the sake of not spoiling this for the others, or ourselves — truce?'

'Hmph.' She thrust his arm away. 'For the sake of the others, yes.'

'Good.'

They arrived at the hotel and the middle-aged woman behind the desk grinned widely at them. She had on a red suit, her thick, black hair pulled up on top of her head.

'Welcome to the Sant'Antonio. I am Signora Perilli.'

Caroline inspected the foyer of the hotel.

'Looks very sophisticated.'

'Yeah, looks good.' Dante was genuinely impressed.

'*Va bene*,' Signora Perilli said. 'I have five rooms booked on the first and second floors, plus the suite on the fourth floor.

'We didn't order a suite,' Anna said.

'Yeah — that would be mine.' Dante put his hand up, like he was answering a question in class.

Anna glared at him and the others didn't seem too impressed either.

'When I booked, it was all that was left.'

'Ah, *si*,' Signora Perilli confirmed. 'I took that telephone call myself. You were lucky we even had that, as it was a cancellation.'

'You've fallen on your feet, doing it last minute,' Caroline said.

'Would you like to swap?' Dante offered.

She patted his shoulder.

'No, you keep it, love. We're only going to use them to sleep in anyway, aren't we?'

He noticed Anna hadn't added any biting comments. Maybe they'd get along OK after all.

When in Rome

Anna was nearly at the front of the queue of pilgrims in the basilica, all eager to touch the feet of its founder, St Peter, when she noticed Dante standing under the dome. The light beams falling from the glass roof on to his head enhanced the sheen of his hair and added a glow to his olive skin. It was like looking at him as a fresh-faced, innocent eighteen-year-old.

He looked in Anna's direction, a smirk plastered on his face. Any brief illusion of his youth was shattered.

Her turn at the statue came. She ran her hand over the smooth bronze feet of the basilica's founding saint, the right set of toes worn almost totally away by the constant stroking of tourists. They were oddly warm.

She moved over for the next pilgrim. Signora Dolci had disappeared from sight with the rest of the students. Anna either had to join Dante or walk around on her own.

'Touching the feet for luck?' Dante said as Anna approached him.

'No. I'm not superstitious. I just like the idea of the history. All those millions of people down the years who've touched the statue.'

He chuckled.

'Put like that it isn't very appealing.'

She tutted.

'Can't you take anything seriously?' she muttered.

'Come on, it was a joke. Lighten up.'

She considered how massive everything in St Peter's basilica was, the dome, the nave, the whole interior space. But it was all eclipsed by Dante's presence.

She looked down at her guide book, reading the lines several times. She wasn't taking any of it in. Walking around on her own was definitely preferable. She strode away to put some distance between them.

★ ★ ★

Dante was entranced by the beauty of the statue he was viewing, trying not to be bothered by Anna's attitude towards him. Man, why didn't she cut him some slack? He'd only been trying to make things light.hearted between them. They'd got on well in those far-distant days. There'd been a misunderstanding, yes. But why did she care about it any more?

'Gloating over the genius of your relation?' a voice interrupted.

He looked round slowly, not wanting to give Anna the satisfaction of knowing she'd startled him.

'Meaning what?'

'Michelangelo's Pietá.' She pointed to the statue of the Madonna and child in front of them.

'I know what it is. What's it got to do with me?'

'Buonarotti. It was Michelangelo's surname too,' she pointed out.

'Was it? Fancy that.' He smiled to himself, looking down at the brochure which he'd chanced buying in Italian.

'Don't give me that! You're not ignorant of Italian culture. And your first name is the same as the greatest Italian writer.'

'Well, my father's responsible for that.' He hoped no resentment had escaped in his voice. 'You and Signora Dolci are the only two who ever refer to me as Dante. Even my mother calls me Dan. And at school you called me Dan too, as I recall.'

'Why are you at an Italian class when you can already speak it?' she asked.

'I've never been fluent. And now I'm exceptionally rusty. My father left the marital home when I was eighteen.'

'Did he?' She looked surprised. But then why would she know anything about it? And the less she knew, the better.

'Yes, to build up his business in Italy.' His words. 'So, here I am, getting in touch with my roots, you might say.'

Dan tried the disarming half-smile that women normally fell over themselves for. Her lack of reaction told him his efforts had fallen on barren ground. She went to move away once more but he didn't want to let her off the hook just yet.

'So, Anna, why did you want to learn Italian?'

'In order to understand the language better when I finally got to revisit Italy.'

Anna walked away and he could have sworn she growled.

★ ★ ★

Anna stepped out from the hotel on to the pavement of the Via Veneto, closing her eyes against the morning sun. Anna thought back to the evening before, sitting in one of the outdoor restaurants down the Via Veneto. They looked like conservatories dotted along the pavement. It had been an evening of relaxation and laughter. Anna had sat at the opposite end of the long table from Dante to ensure this was the case.

Signora Dolci emerged from the hotel.

'Ah, cara, here you are. Now we are all gathered we will make our way to the Pantheon.'

The rest of the party followed on

behind, Dante bringing up the rear with Terry. She had to hand one thing to him — he didn't mind mucking in with people of all ages.

The heat must have defeated even Dante today as he'd abandoned the suit in favour of black jeans and a red T-shirt. Across his shoulder was slung a canvas bag.

'This way, *cari*. About a twenty-minute walk.' The signora pointed westwards, down a nearby side road and marched towards it.

The walk took nearer thirty minutes because of the unscheduled stop to admire Trajan's column. Anna was about to launch into a speech about how it had been built to celebrate a victory by the Emperor Trajan when Dante spoke instead. He told the rest of the party more or less what she was going to say.

'But I guess Anna could tell you more, with her moth — , that is, with her being a history teacher,' he added.

She was sure he was going to say her mother having been a Classics professor but for some reason had changed tack.

By the time they reached the Piazza della Rotonda with its square grey tiles, calming fountain and little cafés, Anna could feel the beads of sweat on her forehead.

Stepping into the cool air of the circular Roman Pantheon, which was now a church, Anna closed her eyes and blew out a sigh.

'Rather spectacular, isn't it?'

She opened her eyes to see Dante indicating they should walk to the middle and she followed him, unquestioning. He stopped underneath the opening in the middle of the dome. Anna did what Dante had done when they first entered, revolving in a complete loop to take in the multi.coloured marble gracing the walls and floor. Then she gazed up at the dome.

'OK, what can you tell me about it?' He was looking at the walls rather than at her.

'Are you mocking me?' she said, narrowing her eyes.

'Not at all. I have to admit that despite coming to Rome with my mother all those years ago, I didn't really bother to find out much about its history.'

'You knew about Trajan's Column.'

'Only because I read it in the guide book last night. I fell asleep before I got to the Pantheon.'

She tutted.

'Shame on you. And you a structural engineer.'

He gave a brief chuckle, the grin that followed forming dimples in his cheeks.

'I know. Woeful.'

'OK. It was originally built in the reign of Augustus and rebuilt by the emperor Hadrian in 126 AD . . .' She stopped there, aware that her passion could well be dull to other people. 'You can read it in your guide book, which I presume you have in there.' She pointed to the bag hanging off his shoulder.

He looked down at it.

'I do, but there's nothing like the personal touch.' Something about the way he said that made her insides fizz. Stop that! It wouldn't do to read too much into anything he said.

They met the signora, giving a talk to the rest of their party, about half an hour later.

'OK, how about we have a coffee in the piazza?' Signora Dolci said. 'Another opportunity to practise our *Italiano*, no?'

She'd had them talking to people in the language since they'd arrived at the airport: the taxi driver, restaurant staff, in a gift shop, asking directions on the street.

Back outside, they found two tables under a large, cream parasol on the sunny side of the piazza, overlooking the yellow buildings on the other side. Dante sat next to Anna.

A young waiter appeared, wearing a black apron, a tea towel draped over his arm, introducing himself as Antonio. His green eyes were quite something against his Latin colouring. He flashed Anna an admiring glance and she enjoyed the compliment.

The signora spoke first, ordering an

espresso. She glanced around her party to invite the next one to speak. Dante went last, sharing a small joke with the waiter which Anna could just about understand. There, another bit of proof that he should have been in a more advanced class.

Caroline's face was alight with mischief after the waiter departed.

'How about teaching us a few chat-up lines, Signora? Antonio is very handsome.'

The tutor suggested some phrases which weren't at all serious. Anna was leaning back in her chair, listening but also taking in the atmosphere of the square. Dante was silent beside her, grinning as Caroline's questions became more outrageous.

'Think you might try one of those lines on Antonio,' Dante murmured to Anna. 'He seemed to be into you.'

'Give over!' she said. 'A holiday fling is not my thing.'

'You're a poet and you didn't know it,' he replied, tipping his head to get a better view her face. 'You look sad.' She stared at his hand, tempted to put hers over his for comfort.

'My mum used to say that to me.'

'You miss her a lot.'

'I do.'

The drinks came and he seemed to retreat into a world of his own. Anna was aware of him at her side, sitting slightly back from her, silently sipping his cappuccino.

'*Bene, cari.*' The signora, looked round to make sure they'd all finished. 'We pay and go to the church of Santa Maria Sopra Minerva. Anna, you ask *il bello* Antonio for the bill?'

'OK.' She was eager to go now. The church in question had been a favourite of her mother's. She looked forward to sharing it with Dante. Well, with the whole group, she added quickly to herself.

Dante stood, placing some coins on the table.

'I think that's what mine cost. Do you mind if I pass on Santa Maria and meet you later?'

'I text you when I know where we eat lunch.' The tutor held up her mobile. 'We see you later then.'

Dante sloped off across the piazza. Anna watched him until he disappeared down a side street. Her heart sank a little. She decided it was because it was nice having someone her own age around, even if it was Dante Buonarotti.

Three Coins in the Fountain

Anna had lost herself in the splendour of the church, looking forward to seeing Dante at lunch. She was disappointed when he replied to the signora's text by saying he would meet them instead for dinner.

Anna was now in her room, choosing an outfit for the evening meal. It was still warm out. She'd brought the yellow summer dress she'd worn that first night Dante had come to class. Stuart had been complimentary about it. She slipped it on, locating her sandals and a cream jacket.

A thought struck her. Dante might not even turn up for the dinner. The same wave of disappointment she'd experienced earlier washed over her. He was good company — when he put his mind to it.

In the foyer Dante was chatting with Terry while sifting through tourist leaflets on a stand. Terry spotted her first, grinning as she reached the bottom step.

'Bella, bella, Signorina Dunlop.' He held out his hands towards her. 'Don't you think, Dan?'

Dante only glanced at her.

'Nice dress.'

'It's the one I was wearing the first night you turned up at class.'

He looked more carefully.

'It's very . . . what's that film set in Rome from the Fifties? 'Three Coins in the Fountain'.' Despite jesting with her he looked tired, his face pale despite his olive skin.

'Very fitting,' Terry said, 'Given we're going to the Trevi fountain.'

When their party was gathered, they walked out into the still light evening. Caroline and Jenny took up position either side of Anna. Dante was at the back of the group with Terry. She could hear the older man talking but didn't detect much feedback from Dante. He'd been in a good mood this morning. At some point at the café, while they'd been drinking coffee, there'd been a switch.

She decided to ignore Dante's negativity.

She was going to concentrate on Caroline and Jenny's cheerful banter.

By the time they entered Piazza di Trevi, Dante felt more inclined to join in the conversation. Caroline and Jenny were telling him about the part of the day he'd missed with them. He wasn't going to put a dampener on the evening, however badly his day had gone. He'd been a fool thinking it might have gone any other way.

Meandering through the crowd, the group started to make their way down the steps towards the fountain. He saw Anna hold back, admiring it from a distance first.

The signora clapped to attract their attention.

'Let us admire the scenery after dinner. I am famished.'

They all trotted back up the steps, following the tutor without question. Dante, at the back of the group as usual, wondered how he might wangle it to sit next to Anna.

As it happened, there was a space next

to her at the round table by the time he entered.

'Did you have a good afternoon?' Anna asked when he'd settled himself.

'Mmm. You?'

'Lovely. You missed a treat at Santa Maria Sopra Minerva. The colours on the ceiling are stunning. And what a day! We've been very lucky with the weather, haven't we?'

The good old British topic! At least it was safe.

'We have.' He recalled the visit here with his mother fourteen years back. They'd had good weather, too, despite it being February. It had helped soothe the first, stressful part of the holiday.

Caroline sighed as a guitarist started singing.

'Ah, would you listen to that. 'Arrivederci Roma', just to complete the romantic mood.'

Dante looked up.

'What romantic mood?'

'We're in Rome, Dan. It's all romantic, isn't it, Anna?'

'Mm? Oh, yes.' She had a thoughtful look, staring at the table until the waiter interrupted her with a menu. Even then she didn't seem to be concentrating on anything.

'A rose for the lady?'

Dante glanced up to see a flower seller pushing a red rose towards Terry, presumably thinking he was hooked up with the signora.

'No, thank you,' Terry said.

'Here,' Dante called, 'I'll have one.' He lifted some coins from his pocket, handing them to the seller. 'Anna, choose a rose.' 'What?' She looked up from the menu.

'Choose a rose.'

'Why?'

'Because I've just bought one and I'm going to look a bit silly with it.'

'Just take a rose and be grateful.' Caroline treated her to a 'What are you like?' expression.

'Right.' She picked a rose. 'Grazie,' she muttered to the seller.

'It's to say sorry for us getting off on

the wrong foot, when I started classes.' He wasn't sure he'd had any particular thought when he'd bought it, but it was as good a reason as any.

'You know those roses are a rip off.' Anna tilted her head towards him, speaking in a hushed tone. Yet she didn't sound displeased.

'Yeah, but sometimes you've just got to do it.'

'Thank you.' She returned to the menu, running her finger down it as she inspected its contents.

★ ★ ★

Anna stepped out on to the side street. It was dark now, the light provided by small lamps attached to the buildings and from shops that were still open. It had been a good evening with pleasant company. That even included Dante. She held the rose in her two hands with her bag. He was only trying to make amends. That was good. She really shouldn't see anything else in it.

110

Dante caught Anna up, walking in silence beside her until they reached the Trevi Fountain. Terry pulled some change from his jacket pocket.

'Hope you've all got a coin. You've got to throw it in, so you come back.'

'No, it's three coins,' Dante said. 'And you've got to throw them with your right hand over your left shoulder.'

'Why's that?' Caroline asked. Anna came up beside her.

'The first is to guarantee your return. The second will bring you a new romance and the third, marriage.'

'Come on, Anna,' Caroline said. 'You might meet a nice Italian boy while you're here.'

'I doubt it, but I'll give it a go if only to return to the Eternal City.' She stood with her back to the fountain, closing her eyes, she didn't know why.

She threw the first coin in, waiting a few seconds before lobbing in the next two and opening her eyes once more. She glanced at Dante.

'I don't suppose you're going to do it.'

'Well that's where you're wrong, Signorina Dunlop. It's tradition, after all.' He took three coins from his pocket, tossing them into the water in quick succession, brushing his fingers together afterwards. He definitely wanted to return, but as for romance? The jury was still out on that one.

So Many Memories

Anna headed down the worn and pitted marble of the Spanish Steps with care, stopping half way down the second flight, holding on to the stone rail. She slumped on to the step beneath her, mimicking others, glad to be out in the fresh air.

It had been a while since she'd had a panic attack, not since the months after her mum had died. The church at the top of the steps, the Trinità dei Monti, had felt oppressive, the walls closing in on her in her imagination.

To one side of her sat a group of teens, laughing and rattling away in rapid Italian. How carefree they looked. There was a young man among them, probably eighteen or nineteen, wavy black hair caressing his neck, his dark eyes bright with life. An intense feeling of déjà vu made her slightly dizzy. He was very like her memory of Dante at that age. When the young man glanced her way, she flicked her gaze forward. She was taking too many trips into the past today.

'Anna?' a voice called from several steps up.

She craned her neck to see Dante taking the steps down in long strides. Part of her wished he'd go away, but another part . . .

Now level with her, he too sat down. 'Why did you run away?'

'I didn't run away. I left quite calmly and quietly. I told Signora Dolci I was going. It suddenly felt . . . ' She pulled a face, not knowing how to complete the sentence. She breathed deeply.

'If you must know, it was the place Mum told me she was ill, the first time.' She'd recovered on that occasion, but some years later, way after the time they all thought she'd got away with it, she . . . she . . . '

'Anna, I'm truly sorry. I shouldn't have come jumping in with my size elevens. I have a hazy memory of you telling us she was ill but I didn't realise how ill she actually was. We must have been, what, fifteen?'

'Fourteen.'

'I'll leave you to your thoughts. As long as you're OK now.' He started to rise and she caught hold of his wrist.

'I don't mind if you stay. I could do with the company.' She took another lungful of air, confirming to herself that the panic attack had passed.

They sat in silence for some moments, watching the to and fro of the tourists. Anna wondered if he was remembering his last trip here with his mother. He hadn't said in so many words, but could it have been to look for his father? She'd surely misjudged him and what she'd thought was his dishonest claim that he'd built up the business himself. For this she was sorry.

He suddenly interrupted her thoughts. 'Anna, there's something I've been . . . '

'*Cari*!' Signora Dolci was scampering down the steps towards them. The students were following on, but a way behind.

'What were you going to say?' Anna asked.

'It can wait.'

* * *

As they entered Piazza Navona that evening Anna was in an excellent frame of mind, even though the fact it was their last night made her sad. It had been a pleasant afternoon with Dante at the Forum, then later at the Coliseum. He had mellowed a great deal during their few days away. She was starting to like the new Dante, or rather, the re-emergence of the old.

Signora Dolci began a tour of the long piazza, mostly in shade now that the sun was on its way down.

'We visit the three fountains.' She pointed to the structures with their statues of water deities, mermaids and beasts.

Having done a complete circuit of the piazza, they ended up back where they'd started, by a restaurant called Il Nettuno. They chose two tables outside, the waiters placing them together specially. Dante scooted round the others in the group to sit next to her. She felt her heartbeat quicken.

Anna recalled the problem of the new shopping centre development back in England. She hadn't thought about it since their first day here. Was he really the villain of her story? For now she'd put it to one side. She'd see if Stuart had made any progress when she got home.

Stuart. Seeing him again would be some reward for leaving Rome.

'You're happy about something.' Dante helped himself to water from the carafe.

'Enjoying the view.' She looked down the length of the piazza, watching as the first lights flickered on.

'Me, too,' he said.

She opened her mouth to ask him what part of the trip he'd enjoyed most, only to find him gazing at her with those intense eyes. The jolt of emotion through her body left her confused.

A waiter appeared with a tray of bite-sized treats for them all and the moment was gone. What had just happened there? Something and nothing, and she should leave it at that.

Caroline was the last to put in her share of the bill.

'Goodness, I can't believe we're going home tomorrow.'

Signora Dolci gathered up the money. 'We still have until early afternoon tomorrow. I know some of you want to buy presents and souvenirs.'

'Does anybody fancy going on to a club? There are meant to be a few around here.' Caroline looked round, hopeful.

Jenny lifted her hand eagerly, waggling it about with the excitement of a child going to a party. It appealed to Anna as well. She had no inclination to end the evening.

'Not for me, *cara*,' the tutor said. 'I am quite content with a simple bar. But do not let that stop you or the others. We do not have to do the same things.'

Dante nodded.

'I'm up for it. Anna?'

A special request for her company?

'Yep, count me in.'

Terry decided to stick with the tutor

and seek out a bar, opting to find one closer to the hotel.

'There's a jazz club round the corner which looks good, according to this.' Caroline held up her guide. 'It's called La Gatta Nera.'

'The Black Cat,' Dante translated. 'Lead the way.' He held out his arm to let the ladies go first.

It didn't take long for Caroline and Jenny to get chatting to a group of middle-aged men — Welsh, as it turned out — there on business. They soon left Dante and Anna at the bar, pulling apologetic faces.

'Looks like it's just you and me.' Dante moved closer to Anna to be heard over the shrill trumpet solo, hoping she didn't mind the change of events too much.

'Shall we get a table?' He pointed to one on a raised area to the side of the bar. He moved in close to Anna again. 'Good choice of Caroline's. I don't get to clubs very often. I used to like dancing when you knew me, all those years back. Remember the parties?'

'You always played Bob Marley at your house. Drove everyone else mad!'

'Yeah, I know.' He laughed.

'You still into reggae?'

'Absolutely.' He regarded her like she was mad to think otherwise. 'And our crowd used to go to that club that played Garage.'

'Lanky's.'

'Yeah, Lanky's. That was it.' A series of memories he hadn't mulled over in a good while came to mind. They'd been a great crowd. Even Stuart, in those days. That reminded him of what he'd meant to tell Anna the other day on the Spanish Steps. Maybe later.

'I sometimes wish I could go back to those days. Things seemed simpler.' He knew he was thinking out loud but was surprised to see Anna purse her lips.

'Did they really?' It was a challenge, but for what reason?

Ah. That. Was it worth raking over it after all these years? Well yes, because it was surely the reason she'd been mega stressed with him.

'Anna, I think I owe you an explanation.'

'No, you don't.' The way she said it, followed by the rapid sip of her wine, suggested she felt the opposite.

'You're annoyed because I stood you up and never explained why, aren't you?'

She looked at the crowd, silent for some moments. Slowly, she rotated her gaze until she was looking into his eyes.

'Go on then, let's hear it.'

Heartless After All

Anna crossed her arms on her lap while her face seemed to empty itself of emotion.

'The afternoon before you and I were due to meet, my father announced he was going to Italy to expand the business, get some new clients. It was very sudden. My mother suspected there was more to it. They had a tremendous row. He left.'

He detected interest in Anna's eyes.

'Anyway, my father had been drinking more and more. The firm was getting less and less work. My mother was keeping us, and it, afloat with an inheritance she got from her grandfather.

'By the time my father went there wasn't a lot of it left. She kept the firm ticking over, bringing in more staff. I worked there while I did my structural engineering degree part time. When I finished it, I was determined to make the firm the success my father never did.'

'That must have been difficult,' Anna said, concern softening the hardness of only minutes before.

'It was.'

'Though I still don't understand why you stood me up.'

'I couldn't face you, Anna. I knew I wouldn't be good company and I didn't want to explain why. I couldn't ring to cancel for the same reason. I was humiliated.' He hung his head, shaking it at the memory of the overwhelming feeling of shame.

'Why would you feel like that? It wasn't your fault.'

He bowed lower over the table.

'He told me I'd be useless, that I'd come to nothing, sponging off my mother's family. Which is what he'd done, basically.'

She moved in closer.

'How could he say that and how could you believe him? You used to get brilliant marks at school.'

'As did he, apparently, along with a first class degree. He said the Buonarotti curse had got his father and it had got him, that it would get me in the end.'

'Oh, Dante.' She took hold of his hands, giving them a little squeeze. 'That's nonsense, and you know it. The fact you've done so well shows that.'

'I didn't believe in curses, Anna, but to make absolutely sure I worked my socks off. Anyway, pathetic as it might sound now, that's why I stood you up.'

After all this time she'd never expected to get an explanation for that evening. It was hard to take it in. She should have realised at the time there was something wrong, that it wasn't like him to be cruel. But he'd distanced himself, played it cocky, probably to cover up the hurt. If only she'd known.

'I really, really wish you'd told me that, Dan. Honestly, I would have understood.' 'The only person I told was Stuart, and even he didn't get the whole story. Though it seems it slowly got round some people.'

'Meaning?'

'Just that people talk, don't they? My

father's clients obviously realised he'd done a bunk. And other engineering firms in the area. Anyway, I don't want to think about that now. I only wanted to try and explain to you why I did what I did. Stupid, since I'd been seriously keen on you for a long time.' He lifted one of his hands, placing it on top of hers.

She had the weirdest sensation, like she was back in the sixth form common room and he'd just walked in, dazzling her with his vital energy. She'd lived for the times she was in his company . . .

'Anna?'

'Yes.' She must have been in the nostalgic trance just a tad too long. 'I'm — staggered.'

'I didn't expect you to feel the same way.

Why would you?'

'I did feel the same way.'

It was his turn to retreat into a stunned silence. When he came to it was to say, 'Do you think we'd still have been together?'

That was an interesting question.

'The chances are slim, what with me going away to uni and you building up your business. Young love rarely lasts.'

Ouch, she'd used the 'L' word.

'You're right. Of course you are.'

Both of them watched the dancers for at least two numbers, before Dante grinned at her.

'Fancy strutting your stuff?'

She giggled.

'Why not?'

It had been an age since she'd danced and it was something she used to love to do.

'I see Caroline and Jenny are dancing, too,' Dante shouted over the music.

They danced to several tunes, the floor attracting more people as time went on. She'd forgotten what a good mover he was, his body at ease with the rhythm. A few songs later, he took hold of her hands.

At one point she caught the eye of Caroline who winked at her, probably getting completely the wrong end of the stick, but Anna didn't care. This was fun, something that had been lacking in her life in the last few years.

'I'm impressed.' Dante moved his lips close to her ear.

'What with?'

'Your dance moves.'

A ripple of pleasure washed over her. She'd been short of this kind of compliment in the last few years, too.

The music slid into a more leisurely tempo. He took her more fully into his arms, their steps slowing to the new beat.

This tune moved effortlessly into another as a spell was wound around her. Dante Buonarotti. How often in the years after they'd left school had she thought about him, playing the what-if scenarios over in her mind until they merged with her dreams.

It had taken a long time for him to disappear from her thoughts. If two months ago someone had told her she'd be dancing with him in Rome now, she'd have thought them daft. Yet here she was.

The lighting softened, reducing everyone around them to dim silhouettes.

Dante pressed his lips together, looking unsure. His face came nearer and he lifted her chin, placing his lips gently on hers. Soft, so soft. It was how she'd always imagined his kiss would be.

But wait! She had a boyfriend. But this is what you wanted, all those years back. Another voice intervened, the one belonging to her sensible self: Are you totally mad!

She pulled away.

'No. This is not a good idea.'

'I — I'm sorry. I thought you were . . . '

'You know I have a boyfriend. What are you doing? Trying to get your own back on Stuart because you don't like him any more?'

'It's not like that.'

'I'm leaving.' She trudged over to Caroline and Jenny, now seated again. 'Hi, I'm going back to the hotel.'

Dante came up behind her.

'As am I. Will you be OK?'

Caroline tutted.

'Sweetheart, Jen and I are old enough to look after ourselves.' 'OK, as long as you're sure.' He caught up with Anna. 'Hold on. I'm coming, too.' 'You don't have to accompany me back.' 'Yes, I do.' They started off down the alleyway. 'Anna, come on. No harm done.' 'I guess you thought I'd be captivated by your charm and forget Stuart, did you?' 'It took you long enough to remember him. Seemed to me you were enjoying the moment. And, well, I didn't think you were actually going out with Stuart properly.'

'Well, I am.'

'Are you sure?'

She stopped abruptly, twisting round to give him what she hoped was her best scowl.

'I saw him, a couple of weeks back,' Dante said.

'You told me that before.'

'In La Gioconda, in Littlebay. Getting very cosy with a leggy redhead.'

Her stomach squirmed, more in humiliation than anything else.

'I've tried to tell you several times,' he said. She recalled the moment at the

Spanish Steps. 'He told me you were just a friend.'

Of course he did. It made sense, the less.than-enthusiastic promise that he'd be in touch, the excuses for not doing so. She believed Dante, but she wasn't going to give him the satisfaction of knowing that.

They walked back to the hotel in silence. Approaching the hotel entrance, his attention was taken by a bedraggled figure skulking in the shadows. That was all he needed, and with Anna as a witness. How could he play this?

'Anna, I'm going to stay here in the fresh air for a while.'

'Do what you like,' she said, not missing a step as she headed under the large canopy for the door.

'Goodnight.'

She didn't reply. For once it suited him that she was being single minded in getting away from him.

He went past the entrance to where the pathetic figure stood, leaning against the wall.

'What are doing here, following me around? We said all we had to say yesterday.'

'I tried to wait in the foyer, but they told me to get lost.' The old man emitted a deep, throaty chuckle that become a chesty cough.

'I don't think there's anything else to be said, do you? You know what's what. I'm keeping away from your tricks.' Dante rubbed his arms. He was starting to feel the cold now he wasn't walking at break neck speed.

'No tricks. You're cruel, Dante, cruel. You owe me, don't you think?'

'No, I don't think.'

'Please.' He clutched the younger man's sleeve.

Dante shook him off.

'Just leave me alone!'

The old man stumbled back, his eyes squeezed shut in pain. Dante blew out a huff of fury at his own stupidity, putting his hand in his pocket to pull out his wallet. He took out several notes and pressed them into the older man's hand.

'Get some decent clothes, for goodness' sake.'

The man pushed the notes into his pocket, shambling off down the road, hugging his coat around him.

Anna had heard enough. She scurried inside before Dante caught her there. She'd noticed the scruffy man in the shadows as she'd approached the hotel. She'd worried about Dante being out there on his own, in danger of being mugged, causing her to linger just inside the canopy. Why had she bothered? Dante had been extremely rude to the poor man who was probably a beggar.

She'd only caught snatches of the conversation, something about the man deserving nothing and Dante implying he was of no importance. Thank heavens she hadn't got herself involved in anything this evening. Dante Buonarotti was cold and uncaring, just as she'd thought when he'd first come back into her life. She should have stuck to that conclusion.

Something Suspicious

'Hi, Stuart, it's Anna.' She'd taken all her courage to ring him up, despite being confident that Dante was trying to cause trouble with his tales of the redhead.

'Anna, how lovely to hear your voice. I didn't realise you'd be back from Rome yet, otherwise I'd have rung you. How was it?'

There, what had she been worried about?

'Lovely. My favourite city didn't disappoint.'

'Good. You managed to put up with Dan then.'

She blushed, remembering how close they'd got and how much she'd enjoyed it. What a fool she'd been.

'Just about. Talking of which, I don't suppose you've heard anything else about that building development.'

There was a pause before spoke.

'Mmm ... Tell you what, why don't we meet up on Sunday for a meal, have a good chat then. Looking forward to seeing you.'

She experienced the heavy weight of disappointment.

'Would you be able to meet up before then, one evening in the week, maybe?' She hoped that didn't sound as needy to him as it did to her. 'I've missed your company while I've been away.'

'I really wish I could but I am up to my ears at the moment with work. I'd like to clear the decks, allow me to relax when I see you.'

That sounded reasonable.

'Of course. I quite understand. Where shall we meet? It's Easter Sunday. It's likely to be busy in town.'

'That's true. I'll come and collect you at, say, ten thirty? Let's make a day of it. We'll take a trip inland, drive round the Downs, find a nice place for lunch.'

That was more like it.

'Lovely. OK. See you then, Stuart.'

'See you, sweetheart.'

Sweetheart! An upgrade from just 'Anna'.

‘This is wonderful. It’s been a long time since I’ve been out on the Downs.’

Anna felt the cosiness of contentment as Stuart’s open topped convertible roamed over the brow of a country lane. Fields of yellow rapeseed appeared either side of them. Her hair flew backwards in the breeze and she breathed in the fresh air.

Stuart pointed up ahead.

‘Here’s the village now.’

The car made a sharp turn up a hill and they passed a sign saying Stouton, before they reached the first house.

‘It’s just up this lane here.’ He turned left, along a narrower road, at the end of which she could spy a large building with a sign announcing *The Half Moon*.

The country inn had a thatched roof and small, leaded windows. Stuart parked, running round to her door to open it while she was still fiddling in her handbag to switch her mobile off. She didn’t want any disturbances over lunch.

'Let's sit out in the garden,' Stuart said. 'What would you like to drink?'

'A lemonade, please.'

'Righty-ho. You go and find us a table and I'll join you in a minute.'

She wandered round to the side of the building, and pushed open the gate to the garden. What a view! The hill beyond the garden rolled down into a valley, with fields and trees as far as the eye could see. She found a table near the outer edge of the garden, sitting so she could enjoy the vista.

Stuart returned with the drinks, placing them carefully on the table He handed a menu to her, then made himself comfortable next to her.

Anna didn't want to keep on about the Adult Education building, but it was an opportunity to get a few answers.

'Have you heard anything else about the proposed development?'

He took a few sips of his drink before replying.

'Yes, been meaning to talk to you about that. I had a discreet ask around but I haven't found out a thing. I'm sure if there was something, someone along the way would know. I believe it was idle gossip, some local news editor raking through the dirt and coming up with rubbish.'

'It didn't only come from the paper though.'

'Oh?' Stuart put down his drink and considered her shrewdly. 'Where else did it come from then?'

She probably should have just left it at that. She didn't want to get anyone in trouble.

'A relation of someone in the Italian class. No idea where she got it from, though.'

'Not from Dan, then?'

'Goodness, no. He seems to be keen to deny there's anything untoward.'

'Does he? Well, like I told you, I'm sure I would have heard if there was anything to hear. Rival construction firms keep their ears to the ground. They have to if they want to secure work. Take Dan, for instance. He always seems ahead of the game the moment jobs go out to tender. He's won a few at my expense from Harper's in the past.'

'Ross Harper?'

'You know him?'

'My father worked for him.'

'Recently?' Stuart looked serious.

'Before he retired, four years ago.'

'Ah. Anyway, I haven't had a sniff of any of his jobs in recent times. Perhaps he just gives them all to Dan.'

Was Stuart trying to hint at something here, that Dante was doing other underhand dealings, even if it wasn't to do with the Community Centre?

'Talking of Dante . . .' she started.

'Do we have to?'

Perhaps he was right. They were having a nice day together and this wasn't exactly going to improve the mood. Still, she needed to get it out of the way, find out where she stood.

'It's just that, while we were in Rome, he told me he saw you in La Giaconda with a, as he put it, leggy redhead. Seemed to think she was your girlfriend.'

'Oh, did he?' Stuart heaved a sigh and plonked his glass heavily on the wooden table. 'That was Hester. She has a firm I do some work for.'

'Apparently you said that I was just a friend.' Perhaps she was. She might have got completely the wrong end of the stick.

'Because it was none of his business.' He raised his eyebrows, inviting her to comment.

'Quite right, too. Enough of him. I bought a present for you in Rome.' She opened her bag, pulling out a smallish bottle containing dark brown liquid and placing it on the table.

'Balsamic vinegar, a decent one by the look. I love this on salad. It was a good choice.' He leaned over and kissed her on the cheek. 'Thank you.'

She lifted up her lemonade.

'Let's drink to an enjoyable afternoon.' He clinked his glass against hers. 'Cheers!'

* * *

Dante considered the distant sea, glinting as if covered with thousands of tiny sequins. He sat at the table on his veranda with his notebook, blessing his good fortune, as he often did. He'd managed to secure this flat overlooking the beach seven years ago.

It had been in a sorry state, putting other buyers off but allowing him to snap up a bargain. Money had been tighter then. He'd done it up over a number of years and it was now just as he wanted it.

The only thing missing was a woman's presence. He hadn't had a girlfriend in the last five months. Not like him at all, but he hadn't had the time or the inclination recently.

The beach was heaving with holidaymakers today, all out to take advantage of an unusually warm Easter. He'd worked on Good Friday and yesterday, wanting to catch up while there were no meetings and no phones ringing.

Today, after a lazy start, he was going to write up the Roman holiday for homework.

As he bit the corner of his bottom lip, considering how to begin, his mobile rang. He picked it up and looked at the screen. The editor of the 'Telmstone Times' clearly wasn't having a day off.

'Hi, Harry, what can I do for you?'

'Hi, Dan. I think both Stuart Keen and Councillor Stacey might be getting a little suspicious.'

Dante sat forward.

'Have they been seen together?'

'Not that I'm aware. Perhaps it's time to speed things up, do what we talked about.'

'Not yet, Harry. If we act too quickly we might not have done enough to be sure.'

'I don't know, Dan. If we leave it too long we might lose the advantage.'

Dante doodled on his notebook.

'Look, I've got someone on the case. I'm still hopeful of revealing something there.'

'Good, good. Just don't let them get in too deep.'

'I'll bear that in mind,' Dante said.

'Perhaps we should meet next week.'

'Good idea. Speak to you soon, Harry.'
He hung up and put the phone on the table, then went back to staring out to sea once more.

A nuisance, but not unexpected. He'd have to sort Stuart out one way or another. He only hoped dear old Terry didn't start stirring up trouble again before he managed it.

★ ★ ★

Anna was at the back of a group of thirteen and fourteen-year-olds, outside the park leading to Telmstone Pavilion. This was the part of teaching Anna really enjoyed, bringing history to life. Once a year they visited the palace, the summer play place of a rich Duke in bygone years.

It might not have the history of ancient buildings like the Forum, but it was impressive in its own way, with its Indian.themed exterior and lavish furnishings.

The group of chattering students came to a halt, prompted by Anna's colleague at the front. Anna made her way forward to speak to her.

'Dee, do you mind if I pop over there?' She pointed across the paved area, to a café. 'I might need some water with all the talking I'll be doing. I'll only be two ticks.'

'Of course, Anna. I'll just give this lot the 'Behave or else' talk.'

'Good luck!' Anna grinned. They were a good bunch, on the whole, but you could rely on one or two of them trying their luck.

Across the road there were people sitting outside in the sun. Inside it was almost empty.

'Hi,' she said as an apron-clad young man appeared through a strip curtain from the room behind. 'Would I be able to buy a bottle of water to take out, please?'

'Sure thing.' He grabbed a bottle from the glass-fronted fridge and took her money. 'Sorry,' he said, looking in the till. 'I just need to get some change.'

He disappeared once more, giving her an opportunity to look round. A couple of middle-aged ladies were chatting and chuckling on a nearby table, while in the corner there were three businessmen in suits. Her throat became dry as one of them twisted around to speak to a colleague. Dante!

And the man on the other side of the table, she recognised him, too. Yes, Harry Fellows, the editor of the 'Telmstone Times'. What on earth were they meeting about?

The third man, the one Dante had been talking to, got up, making his way to the counter, a scowl marring his mature yet still handsome features. Oh, surely not. This got weirder by the second.

When he spotted her he smiled warmly.

'Anna, fancy seeing you here.'

'Hello, Mr Harper.'

'Ross, please.'

She'd never get used to that. Even Dad had referred to him as Ross Harper, when not in his company, never just Ross.

'How's your father enjoying retirement these days?'

'He's got the garden and loves his walking, but I think he misses work a bit, especially since . . . '

'I know. I was terribly sorry to hear about your mother. A real tragedy.'

'Yes, it was. Thank you.'

'Tell Charlie I'll give him a ring sometime. Perhaps he'd like to come and play a round of golf with me.'

She was sure Dad would rather go to a football match any day, but it was kind of Mr Harper, Ross, to think of him. She searched her brain for some way of asking what he was doing here with Dante, but the opportunity was lost when the young guy came back with her change.

'Nice to see you, Anna.'

'Likewise. Ross.' She exited the café, glancing in Dante's direction. He was deep in conversation with Harry Fellows.

Outside she rejoined the school group, following them through the gate and into the park.

Odd to see Ross and Dante together just after Stuart had mentioned Harper's company using Dante's services. And why were they there with Harry Fellows? They might be friends, pure and simple.

Yet she couldn't ignore the fact that the 'Telmstone Times' had recently run an article about the new development, then had retracted it.

Things weren't quite right here. She was seeing Stuart on Saturday. She'd ask him to do a little more digging.

Unexpected Arrival

That meeting with Ross and Harry hadn't exactly been a waste of time, but it hadn't been too fruitful either. Dante was on his way back to the office, making a mental list of the things he had to do that afternoon.

Entering Rachel's office, he saw that she was missing but that the door to his office was ajar. He pushed it open quietly, peering round. Rachel was kneeling on the floor, pulling on the bottom drawer of the filing cabinet, the one he kept locked.

'What on earth are you doing?'

She swung round, her eyes wide with panic. When she saw it was him she relaxed.

'For goodness' sake, Dan. You half scared me to death.'

'The question remains.' He narrowed his lips as he glared down at her.

'I've been looking for the set of calcs you did for O'Brien's, on the old cinema

147

last month. I need to put them with the drawings before Sarah archives them.'

'They were with the calcs the last time I saw them. I keep that drawer locked. It's private, so don't bother trying there in future.'

She pulled herself up elegantly from the floor.

'I'm sorry, I didn't realise. It didn't used to be locked.'

No, but that was before there were things to keep secret. For now. He made an effort to soften his manner. No point taking his irritation out on her.

'I'll look for the drawings later. They might have slipped behind the shelves or something.'

'Thank you. Oh, by the way, a most undesirable fellow called in at reception while you were out.'

'Did he leave a name?'

'No. Just muttered something along the lines of 'Don't you know who I am?' but wouldn't enlighten us. He had shoulder-length hair, grey, wavy and scraggy, an old black wool coat to his thighs. I got

148

Gerry to eject him.'

No, surely not. He couldn't have made his way back to England, could he? The money he'd given him had been a good amount, but not quite enough for that. Unless he'd got a really cheap deal. But who else would it be? He should have known it wouldn't be the end of it. Yet wouldn't Rachel have noticed the likeness?

'Oh, and he had an Italian accent, strangely enough. Sorry, did I do wrong?'

That was the clincher.

'You weren't to know. He — used to work here. Please, if he comes in again, ring me if I'm not in the office.'

The old man was a liability and would probably turn up at his mother's house and upset her. He'd better ring her once Rachel had gone. He should have done it as soon as he'd returned from Rome.

Rachel looked unsure but nodded nevertheless. She turned at the door.

'Are you off to your class tomorrow?'

'Yes. It's the first class of the summer term and I don't want to miss it. Why?'

'I thought you might have had enough after spending a long weekend with them.'

'I'll be going as usual.'

Rachel beamed at him, fluttering her eyelashes twice.

'Just wondered, that's all.'

★ ★ ★

Anna looked over at the classroom door each time someone entered, waiting for Dante to arrive. Not because she craved his company, goodness, no. She only wondered if he'd seen her in the café and whether he'd give any indication if he had.

He was the second to last person to enter, his slim cut jeans and loose T-shirt, making him the most casual he'd ever been in class. Dante, usually at the front, made his way to the back row, at the end, next to her. She opened her mouth to speak, but realised she could hardly object.

The signora examined her watch.

Terry looked round the classroom.

'We're all here, if you want to begin.'

'We wait for one more person. A new lady. She rang yesterday to sign up. Ah, here she is! Signorina Fraser,' the tutor said.

'What!' Dante screwed his neck round to observe the new student entering the doorway. 'Rachel, what are you doing here?'

'Hello, Dan. As you thought so highly of these classes I thought I'd give them a go, since, as you say, we're starting to get business in Italy.'

'This is my PA,' Dante explained.

Anna groaned inwardly. Was she his girlfriend, too? Bit much if she was, after romancing her only ten days before in Rome.

'*Benvenuto, cara.*' Signora Dolci, pointed to a seat in the middle row, next to Terry.

Rachel smiled at the signora, then turned it on Dante, where it became positively foxy. Anna raised her eyes to the ceiling. She was going to have trouble putting up with this for one lesson, let alone a whole term.

'It's this chair next to me, duck.' Terry patted the seat.

Either she didn't hear or she ignored him. Whatever the reason, Rachel headed for Dante instead, taking an empty chair from the table in front, and placing it side on to the end of his table.

The tutor seemed amused as she resumed writing on the board.

'Today, we read back the homework on Rome from those students who were on our trip. I hope this will not be too advanced for Signorina Fraser.'

Rachel smiled coyly but said nothing. Anna wondered if she had any previous Italian knowledge. If not, she was going to struggle in this class which was categorised 'Intermediate'. Her waste of money.

Caroline volunteered to go first, recounting a piece that caused a few intentional laughs, though not from Rachel.

Anna's piece next engendered some

admiring comments, though again, not from the now sour-faced PA who even tutted at one point. She was indifferent to Terry's and Jenny's contributions, examining her nails and parts of the classroom for some of the time.

When it finally came to Dante's turn, it was a different story. Rachel grinned broadly the whole time he was reading, clapping enthusiastically when he'd finished.

'Well done, Dan, well done!'

Anna caught Caroline's eye and they both struggled to keep a straight face.

'In Italian, we say, *Bravo*!' the tutor said. 'Providing it's a man. For a woman it's *Brava*.'

'It wasn't that good.' Dante looked sidelong at his PA.

'But delivered with such passion.'

'Thanks.'

Interesting. Dante was noticeably embarrassed by Rachel's outburst.

★ ★ ★

At break Anna sat with Terry, watching the queue as the rest of the class got their drinks.

'So, what d'ya think of the competition?' Terry eyed her over the rim of his cup before taking a loud sip of tea.

'Competition? If you're referring to Signorina Fraser, I wouldn't mind betting she should be in the beginners' class for a start.'

'That's what I thought, too. Don't think she understood a word.' He sniffed and took another sip.

'OK, what are we thinking? Dante's girlfriend as well as his PA?'

'Nah. I should think he's got better taste than that. You're more his type.'

'Tough luck if I am, 'cos he sure isn't my type.'

Terry chortled and indicated towards the queue. Dante had been served and was coming over with Rachel in tow. Please don't join our table. Please. But Dante did join her table. Rachel looked as put out by the situation as Anna felt, heaving a chair out and pulling it closer to Dante.

'Well, m'dear, what d'ya think of the class so far?' Terry asked as she eased herself closer to the table.

She studied him.

'Good. Signora Dohchay seems to know her job.'

'Dolci.' Anna couldn't resist correcting her.

Rachel pouted.

'Have you done much Italian before?' Terry asked.

'Oh, a little home study, you know.'

'Have you?' Dante looked at her curiously. 'I didn't know that.'

'Before I forget, Dan, would you be able to run me home tonight? My car's low on petrol so I got a bus down. Not an experience I wish to repeat.'

Dante looked briefly at Anna before replying.

'Yes, of course. I'm always willing to rescue maidens in distress.' Another quick glance at Anna revealed a slight curve of his lip on one side.

Oh, yes, very funny. Perhaps she

should ask for a lift, too, cramp Rachel's style. No, being in a confined space with those two would be agony. Best leave them to it.

After the class, Anna watched Rachel and Dante leave the building, her arm linked around his. It saddened her, maybe because it proved once more how much he'd changed over the years.

Tomorrow evening she'd visit Dad, try and get a bit of info out of him on his old boss.

* * *

'You still look a bit pasty, Dad.' Anna placed the casserole dish on the work top in her father's kitchen. 'How are you feeling now?'

'Fine, fine. Stop fussing. I've already eaten, if that's for me.' He heaved himself up to the breakfast bar, slumping against the worktop as he watched her click the kettle on.

'That's all right. You can have it tomorrow, and the night after. Save you cooking. You must have eaten early.' There was no sign that any cooking had been done. He might already have cleaned up — not like him at all.

'I had my main meal at lunchtime. I'll just have some toast this evening.' He rubbed his temple.

'What's up?'

'Just a slight headache. Been sitting indoors too long.'

'Did you go to the doctor to find out what was wrong with you?'

'No point after it's all over, is there? I just need some fresh air, put some colour back into my cheeks.'

'Good idea.' She joined him at the breakfast bar while the kettle boiled. 'There's something I want to ask you.'

'What now?' He sounded peeved.

'It's OK, nothing personal. It's about Ross Harper, actually.'

He looked guarded.

'What about him?'

'When you were working for him, did he use Dante Buonarotti's firm to do structural calcs?'

'Sometimes. I think I told you that before.'

'Yes, sorry. What I meant was, did they use Buonarotti's more than was usual?'

'Not quite sure what you mean. He used them if they put in the best price.'

She tutted.

'Trust them to go for savings, not quality.'

'Don't take that attitude, young lady. It's business. All else being equal, the bottom line's important. Anyway, what's this about?'

'That supposed redevelopment I was telling you about, at the Community Centre. I think Dante might be in on some secret dodgy dealings.'

Charlie frowned.

'And you think Ross Harper's involved, too?'

'Well, I don't know . . .'

'All I know, young lady, is that Ross Harper was a good boss to me. I don't want anything stirred up. He even sent flowers when your mother died.'

She recognised that warning look in

his eyes from when she was a teenager, but she wasn't ready to let it drop just yet.

'I'm not saying he is, Dad. It's just that I saw him in a café with Dante and the editor of . . .'

'And you've put two and two together and made five?' His voice grew louder. 'I don't know what any of this has got to do with you, anyway.'

He started coughing, a deep hoarse cough which had more than a touch of a wheeze about it. Anna stepped forward to rub his back but he got off the stool and moved away.

'You'd better go now,' he managed before coughing again.

'I'm not leaving you like this.'

The coughing slowed, then stopped. Charlie inhaled deeply.

'It's just the leftover from my cold! Now, if you don't mind, my programme's starting on TV in a moment. Bye for now. Take care.' He gave her a cursory hug and a peck on the cheek.

Anna was barely out of the door

before he closed it, leaving her staring at it, confused. That was a weird conversation. She'd hit a nerve mentioning Ross Harper. Still, if her father thought he was the good guy, he was probably right.

She checked the time on her phone. Six-thirty. She'd planned spending a bit more time with Dad and didn't want to go home yet. There was too much going on in her mind. She'd head down to the sea for a walk.

The seashore had always been a place to turn to when she was troubled. Parking up and walking straight to the promenade, she looked out to where the tide was halfway in. She took in several lungfuls of the salty air, staring out to the grey-green sea, gently lapping on to the shoreline.

She'd walked here a lot the two times Mum had been ill. Her mother had been the person she'd often taken troubles to, a sensible voice, particularly during the confusion of her teenage years. When Mum had become ill, she'd been unable to discuss her feelings with her, or with anyone, really.

She so wished Mum was here now to talk over her problems with. First, there was Dante and Rome. Next, the annoying Rachel appearing in her favourite part of the week. And now her dad getting cross with her. Not to mention the worry about the Community Centre. It was all getting to her.

The warm sun encouraged her to go down the steps and take a seat on the lumpy cobbles. Not very comfortable, but it would give her time to gather her thoughts.

As she pushed a stone to one side, she uncovered a worn scallop shell. She picked it up, turning it over in her hands and she felt the sting of tears behind her eyes. It reminded her of those other times she'd walked on the beach as a teen, with her group of friends, including Dante.

He, more than the others, had helped her find interesting shells she could paint. It had been a hobby of hers when she was young.

One blustery day, he'd found her a

particularly fine scallop shell. It had been tempting to give it pride of place on her dressing table, as something he'd touched. Instead, she'd painted Dante's favourite musician, Bob Marley, on to the base of the shell.

Dante had seemed delighted when she'd presented it to him a few days later. In reality, he'd doubtless thought it very girly and chucked it the moment he got home.

As for her problems, Rome was over and she could keep Dante at arm's length. She'd ignore Rachel on Wednesday evenings. She wouldn't mention Ross Harper to Dad again and they'd soon forget their spat. And the Community Centre? She was sure that was all hearsay. There. Sorted.

* * *

Anna turned the page of the essay, sighing heavily at the lines of tiny scrawl. Written at the last minute, by the looks of it. The chatter in the staff room went on around her and her fellow teachers left her to her marking. She really wanted to get it finished so she could get cracking on the Italian homework tonight.

It might also be a good idea to tidy the flat before Stuart picked her up tomorrow.

Perhaps she should suggest picking him up one day, see what his flat was like. Apartment, more like. He lived in the new marina complex that Dante, ironically, had built.

Anna put her brain back into gear and continued marking the essay. By the end of it she had a headache. She placed the paperclip back on the work and slipped it into her bag. As she did so, she noticed a local paper abandoned on the table. It wasn't the one Terry had brought into class, but its rival, the 'Telmstone Echo'.

She glanced at the headline: *Community Centre Up For Grabs?* It was suggesting that the rumours of redevelopment had been hushed, according to an undisclosed source from the planning office.

Had someone been trying to keep things quiet for their own gain? Councillor Stacey had denied once again that any talks had taken place about selling the splendid example of mid 19th-century architecture, as the paper put it.

A quote from a local history group pointed out that their efforts to get the building Grade II listed had been thwarted over the years by the council.

Anna threw the paper down on to the coffee table in disgust. The story here was becoming clearer. Dante had probably been in on this scheme, with some unnamed construction firm angling for the contract.

Councillor Stacey might well be trying to persuade the planning committee to agree. What other explanation was there? And the serious conversation with the 'Telmstone Times' editor? Telling him to lay off. Had Dante bribed him? Threatened him, even?

A cold shiver ran down her spine at the possibility of his involvement. She yearned for the lovely young man she'd known all those years ago, before his father's departure made him bitter and ruthless.

But there was something else. Ross Harper had been in that meeting at the café. Whatever her father said, could he be in on it, too?

Another idea occurred to her, one much more likely. Ross had looked furious when she'd seen him in the café, before he'd spotted her. Was he perhaps trying to warn Dante off, advising him not to get involved?

The only way to find out what was going on was to face Dante, ask him point blank and not be fobbed off.

Anna left school at four o'clock, turning right out of the school gate instead of left. She'd looked at Dante's website again to find out the address of Buonarotti's.

She persuaded the receptionist to let her in with a tale of having made an appointment with 'Dan' that he'd obviously forgotten. He had quite a sizeable operation going on here, with lots of staff. She was shown through to the PA's office, knowing she'd have to face the patronising Rachel. She was right.

'Dan's with someone currently. What's this about?' Rachel indicated where Anna should sit, looking down her nose in contempt.

'Personal business.' If Anna told her she might well be shown the door. Who knew what she was privy to?

'I see. Dan shouldn't be long.'

She sat at her desk, continuing with work, not even offering her a tea or coffee. Anna looked round. Very plush. On the walls were photographs of buildings. She recognised some of them, in particular the aerial view of the marina.

Finally his door opened.

'I'm telling you, I don't know what you're talking about,' she heard Dante say before anyone stepped out.

'The heck you don't, Buonarotti,' another voice, mumbling low, replied. 'If you want my advice, I'd leave well alone.'

The person who emerged was the last person she expected to see.

'Stuart!'

'Anna?' His face reddened as he zipped up the leather document folder he was carrying. 'What are you doing here?'

'Just what I was wondering.' Dante was leaning against the frame in his open doorway, frowning.

'Interesting.' She hadn't meant to voice her thoughts.

'What is?' Dante said.

'Didn't think you two got on any more.'

'We don't,' Stuart said, 'but that's not my fault.'

'Just go, Keen,' Dante said. 'I'm not interested in your — suggestion.'

'Your funeral.' Stuart was soon giving his attention to Anna instead. 'What are you doing here, anyway?' His manner was light, but there was a pinch of irritation, in his eyes if not his voice.

'Italian class stuff.' She'd keep it simple.

'I'll see you tomorrow,' Stuart said. 'Pick you up at six.'

'OK.' Hopefully she'd know a bit more

about the situation by then.

Stuart glanced at Rachel as he left, his lips pursed. She in turn lifted her eyebrows a little.

Dante retained his creased brow until Stuart had vanished.

'Right. You'd better come in, Anna.'

Dante gestured Anna into the office. He glimpsed Rachel's pout as he pushed the door shut. Let her think what she liked. After that performance at class on Wednesday she wasn't his favourite person. That's what you got for being too friendly, he guessed, taking her to dinner, and the other business.

She'd asked him in for coffee when he'd dropped her off last night. He'd politely declined, pleading tiredness. Italian had been an evening off work for him. Now it seemed he'd be taking it with him.

He seated himself at his desk and indicated for Anna to sit opposite.

'To what do I owe this pleasure? Need help with your homework?' He hoped she realised it was a joke. He wouldn't have minded helping her. Pity she was never likely to ask him.

'In your dreams. No, it's this.' She handed him the folded page she'd torn out of the 'Telmstone Echo'. He unfolded it, surveying its contents before throwing it back in her direction. She really was a stuck record.

'And?'

'You said you could guarantee there'd be no redevelopment of the Centre.'

'That's not quite what I said.'

'Stop playing games. Something's going on.'

'Why would you even jump to such a conclusion?'

'I saw you in Café Rosso on Tuesday, with Ross Harper and Harry Fellows.'

That was all he needed! She must have sneaked in because he certainly hadn't seen her.

'And? I know them both of old. Can't a guy meet up with friends, for heaven's sake?'

'The 'Telmstone Times' recently withdrew their story about the redevelopment. Now the 'Echo's' got hold of it.

Ross fed up with your game, is he, and grassed you up to the paper?'

He wasn't going to dignify that with a reply.

'You know Ross Harper, do you?'

'My father was a Contracts Manager of his for many years.'

'Of course he was. I remember now. Ross was a lot of help to my mother when my father left. He gave her smaller jobs to keep her going, then the opportunity to do bigger ones when I qualified and got established.' He'd gone over and above and Dante had a lot to thank him for.

'So you're in with him?'

'I'm not entirely sure what you mean by in with, but I sometimes do work for him. Not as often as I used to because there are plenty of other firms wanting my services. I tender for jobs with Ross fair and square. Sometimes I win them, sometimes not. Sometimes Stuart Keen gets them. All's fair in love and war.'

'But I thought you did a lot of jobs for him?'

'Some, like I told you. Why would you think I did lots?'

For a second, Anna's self assured expression slipped. He glimpsed the girl she used to be, peeping out from behind the fringe, the girl who could light up a dull day. Maybe she was still there, underneath the mask of resentment. What would her reaction be if he asked her out, right now?

Marching to Dante's office in a bad mood seemed like a bad idea now to Anna. Having a feeling something was off wasn't enough. What real evidence was there? Yet it had sounded like Stuart was now warning Dante not to get involved.

Anna wanted to be anywhere but here now, with him gazing at her with those lovely eyes, like he used to in the classroom. She wanted to believe he was innocent, she really did. But she couldn't afford to.

'I'd better be going.'

'Will you meet me tonight, just for a drink? Perhaps we could lay this whole

171

business to rest.' He arched his eyebrows to emphasise the question, a generous smile making a gradual appearance.

He was going to use his charm to make her think he was innocent. How very typical and disappointing. Or was he? Stuart being here earlier had confused the matter. She didn't know what to think now. It was tempting to say yes to the drink, see what he had to say for himself. But it might be a trick to get her on side.

'I doubt it.'

'We had a good time in Rome. It wouldn't be any different.'

'Then it's a definite no, given how that ended.'

'I promise nothing of the sort would occur. I'll take you straight home after. Or you can walk, if you prefer.'

'Thanks, but no thanks.'

'Please yourself.' He looked genuinely hurt. It was probably all part of the game. 'What's made you so bitter against men, Annie?' he asked, as she made to leave.

'It's not men, it's just you,' she retorted.

Before she reached the door a strident voice could be heard coming from just outside. The next thing they knew, the door was flung open and in flew Ross Harper.

Bad News

'Dan, we've got to talk.' Ross Harper held up a copy of this week's 'Telmstone Echo'. His eyes widened and he took a step back as he noticed Anna. 'What are you doing here?'

'Dante and I know each other from school. And we do the same Italian class. We were discussing it.' She doubted Dante would be in a hurry to contradict her.

'I see.'

'Yes,' Dante confirmed, 'but Anna was just leaving.'

What a shame. She'd loved to have been in on this conversation. The fact Ross was brandishing the paper confirmed her suspicions that something was going on.

*   *   *

'Here we are.' Stuart led Anna across the patio of a luxury ground floor flat near the marina. The space was paved, with two tubs containing small palm trees, a pebbled area and an anchor. Even at ground level there was a splendid view of the beach and sea, enhanced by blue sky and golden sun.

'Your place?'

'It is.' He unlocked the patio door, inviting her in.

Inside everything was white or taupe, clean lines with a leather suite and several black and white photos on the wall. Like in Dante's office, they were pictures of buildings. She slipped her shoes off, not wanting to dirty the pale carpet.

'Thought I might treat you to a bit of home cooking.'

Interesting. Stuart had asked her to dress up and she'd assumed they were going for a nice meal somewhere. Furthermore, he'd dressed in a dinner suit.

'Take a seat.' He indicated the nearest sofa before leaving the room.

She sat on the edge of the chair, taking in more of her surroundings. Good quality, expensive. It looked like he'd brought in a designer. Either that or he had a good eye for what went together. The living-room led into a dining area. The table was already laid and included cloth napkins, a pot of roses and two stout candles on glass plates.

'Here we go.' Stuart came back through sporting a crisp white apron, holding a glass of something bubbly aloft. 'I hope you like champagne.'

'Yes, I do.' She reached up to retrieve the drink, taking a sip. 'Very nice, thank you. What do you have on the menu?'

'We're starting with a little chicken liver parfait, moving on to duck confit with dauphinoise potatoes and finishing with chocolate fondant and vanilla cream.'

'Sounds delicious.' Not what she was expecting at all. Good-looking, fun and talented in the kitchen? He got better and better.

Stuart left the room, coming back a few seconds later, minus the apron and with his own drink, and sitting down beside her.

'Everything's under control in the

kitchen, I presume,' she said.

'Of course. Jennifer's a marvel. Don't know what I'd do without her.'

'Jennifer?' He heart sank. Another woman in the house?

'My cook.' He raised a glass, saluting her.

His cook! Wasn't that just a little too — pretentious?

'Is she permanent or just for the evening?'

'She prepares dinner for me every day, unless I'm away or out. Never got the hang of cooking and now I've got the money, why should I bother? She's also my housekeeper.'

The door opened and a woman in late middle age strode purposefully into the room. Her hair was tied up loosely and she wore a large green apron tied round her middle. She was carrying two small plates and beaming fit to burst.

'Here we are, Mr Keen.'

Mr Keen? A bit upstairs/downstairs, surely.

'Ah.' Stuart stood up. 'The first course

is served. 'What a coincidence, seeing you at Dan's office yesterday,' he added as they sat down.

She didn't feel inclined to fib again, and in fact, it was good he'd brought the subject up.

'To be honest, I was wondering whether he knew anything about the article in the 'Telmstone Echo'. It contradicts the article in the 'Telmstone Times' about the development of the Community Centre.'

He looked at first confused, then narrowed his eyes.

'You said it was about Italian class.'

'It was, in a roundabout sort of way. If they pull down the centre and build something else, bang go all the classes.'

'Yes. I can see that.' He took a first bite of the parfait, his gaze remote.

'You did say you were going to look into it.' She was aware her persistence might be starting to sound like nagging.

'What did Dan say?'

She went over the conversation in her mind.

'Nothing, really. Except that he wasn't up to anything with Ross Harper and Harry Fellows.'

He placed his cutlery on the plate.

'Ross Harper?'

'I saw Dante with the two of them in a café, in deep discussion. 'The Times' had recently withdrawn the accusation. I guess I took it all out of context and made up my own story.'

'Or not.'

'Why do you say that? Is it anything to do with why you were there yesterday?'

He looked out of the window, then back at her.

'I saw the article you're referring to that morning. I've recently come to the same conclusion as you, that Dan's involved. I went to his office to tell him he's a fool for getting mixed up with the development.'

She felt a cold sweat break out on her brow. This was not really what she wanted to hear. With all her heart she'd hoped to be proved wrong.

'What did he say?'

'Basically what you must have overheard. He didn't know what I was talking about and urged me to go away.'

'What on earth has he got against you? At school you were best mates.'

'I've no idea, Anna. I'm not aware I've done anything. Perhaps he just doesn't like the competition.'

'You could be right. And as I was leaving Ross Harper arrived, with the same newspaper article I went there with.'

Stuart leaned back abruptly.

'Really?' It was a few seconds before he spoke again. 'I wonder if he went there to talk him out of getting involved, too.'

She thought of her father's insistence that Ross couldn't be involved.

'Now that would make sense.'

'Is there anything else that's made you suspect Dan?'

'Only that he always gets impatient and wants to change the subject when the redevelopment is mentioned. I suppose it's not a lot, but it just seemed odd at the time. That's it, really.'

'It does seem odd. Right, that's enough of Dan Buonarotti for now. Let's enjoy the food and company.'

They clinked glasses.

* * *

Anna sat at the kitchen table with a cup of tea, listening to Sunday morning radio. The dinner last night had been splendid. Jennifer had been a wonder in the kitchen. Sadly she'd also stayed throughout the meal, clearing up the kitchen as they had their coffee.

Stuart had sat close to Anna on the sofa, their bodies almost touching as they'd talked, but he hadn't attempted to put his arm around her or hold her hand, let alone kiss her.

As soon as they'd finished the coffee he'd offered to drive her home. When he'd dropped her off, he'd leaned over for a quick peck on the cheek, and that was that.

She gathered her dressing-gown around her now. His apparent lack of

181

interest bothered her. Might he be worried that she was more interested in Dante? Or was he playing hard to get?

The phone rang and she left the kitchen for the hall.

'Hello?'

'Hello, is that Anna Dunlop?'

'Speaking.'

'This is Telmstone Hospital. It's about your father, Charles.'

Comforting Arms

'Dad, oh, Dad, what on earth has happened to you?' Anna approached her father in the eight-bedded ward, sniffing back the tears she'd been crying in the car all the way there.

He looked very pale, tucked up to his chest in blankets and attached to a drip along with a machine that was taking readings.

'There was no need for you to come running,' he croaked, looking as cross as the last time she'd seen him, when they'd had that stupid argument about Ross Harper. It all seemed pointless now.

'Of course there was need. Look at you.' She tried to tuck the blankets up higher, only to have him fight her off. When he started coughing she stepped back. 'Why didn't you tell me you had flu? Honestly, what are you like?'

'I didn't know I had flu. Still don't know if I did. The doctor thought I might have had, but then it . . . ' He stopped, panting a couple of times.

'Don't talk. It doesn't matter.'

'I'm fine.'

'You are not fine! And I know what you were going to say. Because you didn't go to the doctor to get your flu seen to, you got pneumonia.'

'Like I said, I didn't know it was that. I thought it was . . . Well, I didn't want you to go through with me what we went through with your mum.'

'Oh Dad!' Her chin wobbled and she couldn't stop the tears from falling. 'Ignoring it wouldn't have made it go away.'

'Guess I wasn't thinking straight. Felt a bit weird, to be honest.'

She remembered their argument once again, the unreasonable behaviour which was not like him.

'You were acting a bit weird, too.'

'I know. Sorry about the quarrel. Don't know what I was thinking.'

'It's all forgotten. You're in the best place now. They'll look after you.'

'Have you heard anything more about

the development?'

She peered round at the other occupants, not wanting what she had to say to be overheard.

'Well . . . ' Was it fair to burden him with this? He'd only stress out about it if she mentioned Ross again, even though it was unlikely he was involved. 'I guess it was something and nothing. The local papers got the wrong end of the stick. That's all.'

He graced her with a weak smile. 'I'm glad to hear Ross Harper's not involved in anything dodgy after all.'

After all? As if it was possible he might have been? A bit of a change from what he'd claimed before.

'I was glad to retire, you know, when the opportunity arose. Apart from spending time with your mother.'

'Yes, it was a godsend that you were able to take early retirement.'

'It all got a bit too political for me.'

'What did?'

'The building industry. I'm not surprised there's something going on with the Community Centre.' He paused to catch his breath. 'I'd be surprised and disappointed if Buonarotti's was involved, though. Still, who knows these days. People get greedy.'

Back in her car in the hospital car park, Anna texted Stuart to tell him about her father. She needed a sympathetic ear and half hoped he might offer to meet up, or ask her round, to cheer her up.

She didn't want to push it, though. He'd told her the previous evening, when he'd dropped her off, that he'd be busy with work for a few days. She probably wouldn't see him till the next weekend. If only she knew where she was with him, whether there was an actual relationship here.

There, all sent. The drive home would take ten minutes. Hopefully she'd have a reply by then.

But the reply didn't come until six hours later, when she was about to head out to the car for evening visiting.

Sorry to hear that. Let me know how he's getting on. Take care. xx

So much for the sympathetic ear.

'What on earth is wrong with you?' Caroline called, before Anna had even taken half-a-dozen steps into the classroom. 'You look peaky as anything.'

'Do I?' she said, though she didn't doubt it.

Her father, a little better but bored to tears, had been muttering about discharging himself from hospital when she'd been there earlier that evening. He was nowhere near well enough. She'd had a word with a member of staff. With any luck the hospital would talk him into staying put.

'Come and tell your auntie Caroline all about it.'

Dante strolled in, his books under his arm.

'All about what?'

'Look at how pasty she is.' Caroline stroked Anna's arm as she sat next to her.

Dante sat the other side of her.

'Caroline's right, you're white as a

sheet. What on earth is wrong?'

'My father . . . ' She took a couple of breaths before continuing, to make sure she wasn't going to embarrass herself by bursting into tears. 'He's in hospital with pneumonia.'

Dante took her hand.

'Oh, no! How is he?' Caroline cried.

Anna took another deep breath.

'Out of danger, but it could have been so different.' She explained about the untreated influenza and how he'd got annoyed with her when she'd gone round. She tried hard not to be distracted by the warmth of Dante's hand on hers.

'But he's going to be OK?' Dante asked.

'Yes. Providing he stays put.' She went on to explain the follow up ordeal this evening.

Dante placed his other hand around hers, encircling it.

'Why didn't he tell you he felt so rough in the first place?'

'Well, that's the thing. He was afraid

he might have something more serious. Like my mum did. He didn't want to be a burden on . . . '

The sniff she intended became a choke. Before she had a chance to get a grip on herself, the tears began to pour down her face.

'Oh Anna,' Dante said, a moment before he removed one hand and placed it round her shoulders instead.

Without any conscious thought, she burrowed into his chest, her body enclosed as he brought his other arm round. She felt such peace in his arms, like his embrace could solve all her problems. It would at least soothe them for a few moments.

She heard a muffled, 'What's up?' which she recognised as Jenny's voice.

'Anna's father's ill,' Caroline explained. 'Dan, why don't you take her into the empty classroom next door, before everyone else gets here?'

She felt herself lifted to her feet before being led into the corridor and into the next room. Dante put the light on and they moved away from the partly glass door. Standing in front of the whiteboard, his arms surrounded her once more, pulling her in close to him.

The problem of the redevelopment flitted into her mind. Forget it, she told herself. At least for now. She needed this comfort. How could a man so compassionate, so gentle, be capable of conniving, underhand tricks? He couldn't. And that was good enough for her at this moment in time.

Dante lowered Anna's head on to his shoulder. All those fiery emotions that he'd experienced during his teen days, the affection he'd felt for her, came flooding back. Affection? No, more than that. Love.

He'd fallen in love with her the moment he'd met her in the first year of secondary school. It had only grown as the years had gone by. Yet he'd been incapable of even asking her out, until that last day in the sixth form.

What a total fool he'd been, standing her up. His idiotic pride had got in the way, not wanting to show how his father's betrayal had hurt him.

Even now there was a barrier in their way. The blasted redevelopment. The sooner he sorted that out and was able to explain it to her, the better. Whether she'd ever trust him after what had gone on between them, he didn't know. He could only hope. For now, he'd be a shoulder for her to cry on, someone she could talk to. That would be a good start.

Dante had waited until Anna was all cried out, before letting her go.

His arms had been so comforting but nothing good lasted for ever, did it? Or so it often seemed to her.

'I'm fine now,' she croaked as he stepped away from her.

'No, you're not. Look, would you rather I collected our things and we go for a coffee? You don't have to face the others.'

It was tempting to have him all to herself but she didn't want him to feel obliged to look after her.

'It's all right. We can creep in so as not

191

to disturb the lesson.'

'Would you like some water from the cooler?'

She nodded.

'Thank you. Some water would be great.'

Crying, she decided, must be thirsty work, as she drank down the water he brought her in one go.

'Ready?'

'Ready as I'll ever be.'

As they were about to reach the door of their classroom, she lay her hand on his sleeve to stop him.

'Thank you, Dante, for, you know, looking after me.'

'Any time.'

Their eyes met. He looked concerned. She found it difficult to pull her gaze away. He was like a magnet and if she wasn't careful, she'd be compelled to wrap her body around his again. She was struggling to breathe, her heart was pounding so fast.

'Are you sure you're OK?' he said.

She dragged her eyes away, checking the time on her watch. She realised then she was shaking, so quickly hid her hands behind her back.

'Sounds quiet in there. They must be doing an exercise. It'd be a good time to creep in.'

He opened the door. Her time alone with him was over. She felt as relieved as she did disappointed, covering both emotions with a poker face as they found their seats.

★ ★ ★

People inevitably made a fuss of Anna during the break time, after hearing the news about her father.

The only person who didn't was Rachel. Not that Anna was surprised. She could have done without the pouting and sighing, caused, no doubt, by everyone's lack of attention to her.

'People are kind, aren't they?' Anna said to Dante as they took their empty cups back to the counter after the break, the last two students to do so.

'Most are, if you give them a chance.'

Did he mean himself? She had been hard on him when he'd first arrived in class.

She'd taken her disappointment and fury at being stood up all those years ago, and squashed them into a weapon to beat him with. Bad of her, who would have advised anybody else to see what he was like now, before jumping to conclusions.

'I'm sorry.'

He looked confused.

'What for?'

'For being off with you, when you started the Italian class.'

'Oh, that. Forget it. It's not important.' He was about to open the door for her. 'If you need someone to talk to in the week,' he added, 'give me a ring, or text me.'

'I don't have your number.'

'Here.' He scooped his phone out of his jacket pocket. 'Let's exchange numbers. And let me know if you need a lift to the hospital or anything,' he added after they'd keyed in the numbers. 'You might not be feeling up to driving.'

'OK. Thanks.' She went ahead, afraid she might start blubbing again if she looked too long at his anxious face.

★ ★ ★

Charlie had his eyes closed when Anna came in with a bunch of bananas, a carrier bag of novels and a gardening magazine — the third she'd bought that week. Her father had lapped them up. The suggestions given to her by her fellow students, to keep Dad in hospital, had been worth their weight in gold. Along with the magazines, she'd found two gardening DVDs online. She'd brought them in along with her old laptop.

She'd also downloaded classical music for him on to an MP3 player — Dante's suggestion. At first he'd scorned what was, to him, new technology. He couldn't get enough of it now and she'd had to download more. The two puzzles had proved popular. One was half done on a tray, sitting on his overbed table.

So far there'd been no more talk of discharging himself. She placed the new items quietly on his bedside locker before lifting a chair at the end of the bed to bring it closer to his face.

'Hello,' he said, without opening his eyes. 'Thanks for the bananas.'

'How do you know I've brought you bananas?'

'I can smell them.' He did now open his eyes, trying to pull himself up straighter on his three pillows.

'Hold on, I'll give you a hand.' When she'd finished the task, she smoothed out his blankets for him. 'You've got a bit more colour in your cheeks today. Have you been eating?'

'I have. Ask the nurses if you don't believe me.'

'I do believe you. I went to your house, just to tidy up, and I noticed you hadn't eaten any of the meals I made for you. They're all still there in the freezer, along with that casserole.'

'Sorry.' He looked genuinely regretful. 'I really lost my appetite. At least they'll be there for me when I get back.

'Oh, by the way . . .' Anna reached into her handbag. 'This card arrived at the house. I think it's a card.'

Charlie opened it, looking serious.

'It's from Ross Harper wishing me a speedy recovery.'

He placed it flat on the locker. Anna looked inside, then stood it upright. So much for not bringing his name up.

* * *

The sun was still reasonably high in the sky as Anna walked to the Italian class. She was glad she'd changed into a shorter skirt than she'd been wearing for school, swapping her blouse for a sleeveless T-shirt.

She passed through the Alleys, a series of lanes with independent and alternative shops, a slightly longer route to the Community Centre, but a more entertaining one.

As with every other evening, she'd been to the hospital. The colour was returning to her father's cheeks more with each visit, and he was able to move about a little better.

Because he'd fretted about his garden becoming too overgrown, she'd mown the lawn over the weekend and snipped back the hedges. Dad's garden was his pride and joy. She didn't want him going back to disarray and getting despondent.

Anna emerged out of the alley into an open space where there were several cafés and a pub. She checked her watch. Only another three or four minutes and she'd be at class, ten minutes early. Great.

Ahead of her she spotted a familiar tall, slim figure. It was Dante, in blue jeans and a light blue T-shirt. It amused her that he was walking, not driving that impractical, if beautiful, sports car.

It was reassuring to know he appreciated a stroll on a sunny, warm evening, like her. She should catch him up, enjoy the last stage of it with him.

He had been incredibly supportive

during the week, texting every day. He'd certainly done a better job of keeping her spirits up than Stuart. What on earth was she going to do about him? Accept it had come to an end?

Anna put a spurt on, determined to catch Dante up. At least his PA wasn't with him. Dante made his way down another lane now, one filled with shops and cafés, which led to the main road. A man jogging beside him started talking to him.

He was shorter than Dante, dark, bedraggled. He wore a long, black wool coat, incongruous in the current temperature. The two of them stopped half way down the lane, facing each other. The old man put his hands out, his face contorted into a pleading desperation.

Dante was clearly irritated with the man. It took her back to that last night in Rome, outside the hotel, when he'd been rude to the beggar. Dante pointed his finger at the man. She couldn't hear the content of his speech, but she could tell it was a rant. Poor old chap, what had he done?

She took a moment to decide, then ran towards them, worried for the old man's safety. Just when she was warming to Dante, he proved once again he didn't deserve it.

As she reached them, Dante spotted her.

'Just go!' he shouted to the old man. The man gave Anna a quick glance before scampering away.

'Please, Dante, think about it,' he turned to call.

He knew Dante's name?

'What are you doing to that poor old man?' Then something occurred to her. She could be wrong, but it made sense, and all her suspicions were back. 'Is that your mole?'

'My what?' He narrowed his lips and his eyes at the same time. 'What on earth are you talking about?'

She wasn't sure herself, but blundered on regardless.

'Your mole, from the planning committee, maybe? Making sure you get the redevelopment package?'

That wasn't how she'd meant to say it. She was handling it all wrong. Perhaps the man was trying to get Dante involved in something untoward that he wasn't interested in.

'Not that again! Didn't you recognise the accent?'

'I, um . . . ' She recalled the old man's words. 'Italian?'

'Exactly!' He clapped his hands against his sides, walking away then back again. Leaning down towards her, he said, 'My father, Anna. My father!'

Unpleasant Scene

'That was your father?' Anna was shocked. He didn't look at all like the man she'd glimpsed now and then as a teen.

'I went to meet him in Rome, that afternoon you all went to Santa Maria. Disastrous. I should have known better.' He was raking his hand through his hair. 'He was waiting for me at the hotel on that last night. You might have seen him.'

The old tramp, or so she'd thought. She hadn't got a good look at him then.

'I made the mistake of giving him money. He used some of it to catch a flight back here, to get some more. I gave too much away about how successful I've been, wanted to show him I'd done OK without him. I should have left well alone.'

'Dante, I'm sorry.'

'Save it for someone who cares what you think.' He stormed off.

Anna pushed open the door of the class-room, not expecting to see Dante there. She was right. Only Terry and Caroline were present, talking very seriously on the other side of the room.

'Hi,' she said, as she took a seat.

They greeted her back briefly, barely breaking from their muffled conversation. Soon after, the rest of the students filtered in, plus Signora Dolci. There was still no sign of Dante, and she didn't expect there would be. What an idiot she was. But even if she hadn't intervened, he was so wound up about seeing his father, he surely wouldn't have attended this evening.

Rachel entered next, inspecting the room. Her pinched mouth indicated she wasn't happy with what she saw. She'd be disappointed if she was waiting for Dante.

Or not. He sauntered through the door, face neutral, not greeting her or Rachel and only lifting his hand when the tutor spoke.

Rachel wasted no time in following him, taking the seat beside him.

The tutor continued, seeing that everyone was now present.

'First of all, I have some news. I am not sure how official this is, but I feel I should share it with you. The Italian classes, in fact, all the classes, are going to be reviewed. That is to say, some may not start again in September.'

'Just as I thought!' Terry blurted out. 'They're going to pull down the building, aren't they?'

'I am not sure if that is the case . . .' the signora started.

'Well I am,' Terry said. 'My daughter Megan told me there'd been whispers of backhanders. Developers and structural engineers have been poking their snouts in to bully the planning committee into selling this building for redevelopment. It belongs to the people of Telmstone!' He thumped the table with his fist.

Dante stood up abruptly, his chair banging against the table behind.

'Who's been opening their big mouth?' he shouted.

Terry rose to his feet, pulling himself up to his full height and puffing his chest out.

'Oh, then you do know about it?'

'I know it's a pile of misinformation.'

'So you say!' Terry pointed his forefinger accusingly. 'Are you the developer?'

'I'm a structural engineer, Terry. I only work for developers.'

'Then I bet you're on a promise of some work.'

'Now, now, cari.' Signora Dolci raised her voice to no avail.

'You're as bad as they are!' Terry hollered.

'Yeah!' Caroline said, rising and screwing her face up. 'It's all money, money, money with your sort. I've seen that car you drive.'

This was getting out of hand. Anna was next to stand up.

'I think we should all calm down. Give Dante a chance to explain what he does, or doesn't know.' She was willing, for the time being, to give him the benefit of the doubt.

'Well, lad?' Terry crossed his arms tightly across his chest.

Dante was about to open his mouth when Rachel stood, her face flushed.

'How dare you talk to Dan Buonarotti like that. Who do you think you are, nasty little plebs, shouting accusations all over the place when you know nothing?'

'Rachel, please stop,' Dante pleaded.

'Plebs, are we?' Caroline left her chair and scooted round the table to face Dante's PA. 'I'd rather be a pleb than a puffed up secretary chasing around after her boss.'

'Dan has nothing to do with the redevelopment, I can assure you of that.'

'Yes, like your word counts when you're clearly smitten with him!' Caroline had got that right, at least.

Anna needed to work out what to do for the best before this turned even nastier.

'I think we should all . . . ' she started.

Rachel rounded on her.

206

'And you can just shut up!'

'Oh, shut up yourself!'

'Hear hear!' Caroline said, with a mutter of agreement from the rest of the students.

Dante coughed to get their attention.

'If I can just explain.'

'We're all ears, lad,' Terry said.

Let him get a word in edgeways, Anna thought, wishing they'd all just be quiet and listen. She wanted to hear his explanation too.

'Don't you take that attitude,' Rachel barked, screwing up her face.

Terry tutted.

'Don't you talk to me like that, young lady.'

'I'll talk to you . . . '

'Enough!' the signora boomed, in a voice Anna had never heard her use before. 'This is not the place for this discussion. Dante can explain to you all at break.'

'I want to hear now,' Terry persisted.

'I forbid it!' Signora Dolci stamped her foot.

'You know what?' Dante said. 'I'm really not in the mood for sharing.'

He picked up the shoulder bag, placing his books back in it, and sprinted to the door.

'Dan, wait for me.' Rachel gathered up her things and ran after him.

He swivelled round, tight-lipped.

'Rachel, I am not in the mood for you, either. You've only made it worse. Just leave me alone, please.'

She stood, open-mouthed, watching him leave. Some seconds later she looked back at the students.

'Well, I'm not staying, either. You're all, you're all — horrible!' With that, she strutted out.

Great, just great. Well, let the two of them sort it out. Anna had had enough now. She sat back down, tight-lipped, opening her books.

The signora wrote the date on the board in Italian.

'Now, no more talk of anything but l'italiano until break time. A quick exercise.' She wrote some sentences on the board, with missing words that they were required to fill in.

Anna remained staring at the first question, the events of the evening, both before and after she arrived in the class, crowding her mind. How was she going to make it right with Dante? And what on earth was he going to tell them earlier?

After ten minutes, Anna rose, packing her books away without any conscious thought about why she was doing it or where she was going.

'What is it, Anna?' the signora asked.

'I can't continue tonight. Really, you were all appalling,' she said, stopping to give them a look that left them in no doubt she wasn't joking. 'If you'd just let Dante speak without interrupting and jumping to conclusions. Honestly.'

As Anna strode across the room, Caroline called out.

'I'm sorry, but it did all seem rather a foregone conclusion.'

'Only to you lot.' Anna opened the door to leave.

'But . . .'

'Let her go,' she heard the tutor say. 'It is best for now.'

Pushing open the outside doors, Anna marched into the street. She stopped to consider what to do. She was too out of sorts to go home. Maybe ring Dante up or go to his house, find out what he was going to say? She needed to know.

She headed across the street and back up the lane where she'd seen Dante talking to his father. As she approached the end that led into the square, she became aware of a man and a woman, sitting on the opposite side, outside a pub. The man was looking round at the crowds uneasily. They were deep in a troubled discussion.

It was Rachel and Stuart.

Dirty Tricks?

'Anna, like I explained at class, I'm not in the mood. Let's do this some other time.' Dante, phone in one hand, pushed his front door open with his free hand, glad to be in the sanctuary of his apartment.

Hearing Anna's voice would normally be near the top of his list of the best things in life, but just now he was exhausted. This situation had been going on far too long. He wanted to know for definite what was occurring before he brought it to a close.

'But your PA is outside the pub with Stuart having a serious conversation. She's up to something.' Her voice on the other end of the phone was agitated.

'Yes, I know she is.'

'You know?'

'And I'd rather you didn't approach them, otherwise weeks of work will go down the pan.'

He held the phone away from his ear

as she shouted.

'What — is — going — on?'

'Please Anna, trust me.'

'Oh, hang on.' He heard a rustling and some street noise. 'Sorry, had to hide in a doorway. They just went past. I'm going to follow them. They've turned right at the end. That could mean they're going to his place.'

'Anna, no.'

'I'll let you know what I find out.'

The phone went dead.

'Anna. Anna!' Dante heard himself yell, though he knew it was useless.

Right, there was no alternative. He threw the bag on to the sofa in the living-room, grabbing a lightweight jacket before leaving his home once more. He only hoped she was right about their destination.

* * *

She had been right. Stuart and Rachel were now entering the marina apartment complex, still speaking in irritated bursts, much hand waving in evidence. There was a whole other situation going on here that demanded an explanation, but she wasn't going to get anything out of them by storming over and asking.

Had Dante found it hard to explain things this evening because it involved Rachel? Rachel, whose boss had no love for the man she was now in discussion with? The woman had done her best to cause uproar and prevent Dante from speaking at class. It would be a jolly good explanation for it.

As they approached the gate to Stuart's patio area the two of them stopped. Anna was able to edge nearer, sheltered by a tree with low branches.

'This is all your fault, and I'm going to prove it!' Rachel poked Stuart with a forefinger.

'I'm still not entirely sure where you're going with this. I've only invited you here in order to discuss it in private, not with half of Telmstone looking on. But I'm not going to be shouted at.'

'Oh, aren't you? Well I'll come to the

point. It's you who's been putting up the money to bribe Councillor Stacey and his fellow councillors on the planning committee, so you can pull down the Community Centre. And now Dante's getting the blame for it.'

'You what? You've got this completely backwards.'

'I don't believe I have.'

Then it was Stuart who stood to profit from the dirty dealings? Anna's brain was spinning with the possibilities. Or it could be a double bluff, to confuse the matter. Perhaps she should record this. She shuffled around in her bag and found her phone.

While she was looking for the voice recorder function, the phone slipped and flew out of her hand, landing several feet away. The sound alerted Rachel, who spun in her direction as she scampered to retrieve the phone. She attempted to dart back behind the tree but she was too late.

'What are you doing here?' Rachel shrieked.

Stuart closed his eyes and slumped against his railway sleeper fence.

Now she was exposed, she had no choice but to tackle them. She came out of her hiding place, walking confidently towards them.

'I could ask you the same,' Anna said. 'I'm fast coming to the conclusion that I can't trust either of you, but I'm guessing one of you is telling the truth. The question is, who's the guilty party, Dante or Stuart?'

'Well, it isn't me.' Dante appeared from around the corner, the ring of his car keys looped round a middle finger.

'The devil it isn't,' Stuart said. 'It's not me. And why else would you send Rachel to keep an eye on me but to keep me off the scent of your dirty tricks?'

'That wasn't the reason!' Rachel yelled.

Stuart sneered.

'I'm not completely stupid. I know you weren't befriending me and flirting with me for my boyish charm. How long did it take you to track me down in that club, before you came sidling up to me? 'Oh, Stuart, I've been dying to meet you properly for ages.' Give me a break.'

It was hard not to laugh, so well had Stuart imitated Rachel's rather nasal tone.

'But I have to hand it to you, Rachel, I didn't suspect your motives until Anna planted the seed of doubt in my brain. Especially when she wouldn't let it go and I found out Dan was making enquiries.'

'It was important,' Anna said, defending herself.

'Indeed,' Dante said. 'But Rachel didn't befriend you to keep you off my back, Stuart. Quite the opposite. It was to find out what you were up to.'

Stuart had a look of amazement on his face.

'You thought the underhand dealings were being done by me?'

'Who else? You're a chip off the old block. Like father, like son.'

Stuart bounded forward. Anna jumped between them, halting his progress.

'Meaning what, exactly?' he shouted.

OK, this was going in a direction that Anna couldn't have predicted in a month of Sundays. Either one of them was lying, or neither. She was hopeful for the latter, but what if they were both involved, trying to keep the other at bay?

Dante took a while to reply. When he did, all emotion had been wiped from his expression and voice.

'What your father did to my mother. Or tried to do.'

'I'm still at a loss to know what you're talking about.'

'Your father, taking advantage. I told you in confidence that my father had left us, yet somehow your father found out.'

Stuart's anger melted from his face, replaced with something bordering on compassion.

'He didn't hear it from me, Dan. To be honest, I think it was common knowledge among the construction firms. But what's that got to do with anything? And is that why you've barely spoken to me in fifteen years?'

Dante's face paled at first before he pulled himself up tall, defiant.

'I guess it must be. Your father hassled my mother to let him buy her out, at a rock-bottom price. Told her she'd never manage on her own.'

'I promise you, Dan, I knew nothing about that.' Stuart looked truly troubled by the revelation. 'It's still a leap, from something that happened fifteen years ago to thinking I'm taking backhanders to get a big job.'

It was Dante's turn to look troubled.

'Ross Harper suggested it might be you. I assumed he had some insider information.'

Stuart shook his head.

'The Ross Harper who's frozen me out of contracts recently that I was perfect for? The Ross Harper who threw my company off a job not long ago for some trumped-up reason? Oh yes, it's starting to become clear now.'

Rachel tossed her hair back.

'I'm glad it is clear to you.'

For once, Anna agreed with her.

'The Ross Harper,' Stuart went on, 'who was totally besotted by your mother at one time, Dante, and was upset the feelings weren't reciprocated?'

'But, but . . .' He struggled to speak, his face drawn, guarded, like it had been in the weeks after he'd stood Anna up.

Dante never finished his sentence, simply looking at the ground, defeated. Rachel went towards him, her arms outstretched. Before she reached him, he put a hand up, palm out, halting her in her tracks.

'Let me get this straight,' Anna said. 'Stuart, that day you went to Dante's office, when I showed up after you — didn't you sort out then that neither of you was involved?'

'I thought Dante was pretending ignorance because he already had the job in the bag and didn't want any competition.'

'And I thought you were warning me off because you were interested in the job,' Dante said.

'Honestly, men!' Rachel shook her

head and tutted.

'One more thing,' Stuart said, addressing Anna. 'An apology for leading you on. You're a lovely girl, but I really only want to rekindle our friendship, not anything else. I thought my taking you out might give me some information on Dan.'

'You thought I was involved?'

'No, just that you might know something that would be of interest. I'm already seeing someone.'

'The redhead, by chance?'

He had the good manners to blush.

'Hester, yes. Sorry.'

She should have been outraged, being used in that way. Or upset. Or something. She searched for some kind of reaction within her. No. Nothing.

'Apology accepted. No big deal.'

The awkward moment was saved by Dante's mobile, ringing from his pocket. He fished it out, looking at it with a brief frown, before putting it to his ear.

'Hello, Harry. What can I do for you?'

Harry Fellows, the editor of the 'Telmstone Times'? Hopefully he'd have more information on the situation.

'Whaaat?' Dante's yell ended on a high-pitched note. 'You are kidding me. Right, right. For goodness' sake! OK, We'll be down . . . Yes, we, four of us. I'll explain when we get there.' He pressed a button and replaced the phone in his pocket. 'That was Harry from the local rag.'

'I think we'd gathered that,' Stuart said. 'What did he have to say?'

'There's a crowd gathering outside the office, protesting about the redevelopment.'

Never Too Late

'We'll go in my car, since I have it here,' Dante said, leading the way to the car park.

'You're shaking. I'll drive,' Anna murmured so the others couldn't hear. He frowned at her initially. Worried about his precious car, no doubt. But his posture relaxed and he handed her the keys, going round to the passenger side. Stuart and Rachel got into the back, neither saying anything.

Anna surveyed the controls, wondering whether this was such a great idea. She'd driven Dad's little sports car, one he and Mum had enjoyed gadding about in after he'd retired, and before she'd become too ill. It wouldn't be as powerful as this, though. But everything looked pretty standard. She started it up and was relieved to move off slowly, without any jerks.

She noticed Dante lift his phone and put it to his ear. Looking in the mirror before she signalled to turn left, she noticed Stuart do the same. Both, it transpired, were talking to parents, as she heard the words, 'Mum,' and then, 'Dad,'. Whatever was said after that was muffled.

Amongst the crowd of around 200 people outside the office of the 'Telmstone Times', Anna spotted most of the Italian group. Only Signora Dolci was missing. They must have left the class early as it was only just eight-thirty now.

Terry was holding aloft an A3 sheet of paper with *SAVE OUR COMMUNITY CENTRE* written on it in red felt pen. Even dear old Ellen was there. A confused mix of inaudible chants were ringing out, one lot led by Caroline.

'Must be a strong feeling against the development, if a crowd this big can be gathered at short notice.' Dante displayed no surprise.

Terry spotted them as they pushed through the front of the crowd, shouting Dante's name and something else she didn't hear. There was no time to stop now and it wouldn't be a good idea in any case. She was relieved when they reached the office and were behind a closed door.

Standing with Harry Fellows behind his desk was a young woman, petite and in her early twenties.

'Well, this is a turn-up,' Harry said, leaning his knuckles on his desk.

'What's with the mob?' Dante had recovered his composure during the course of the journey.

'Decided I wasn't going to keep quiet any longer,' the young woman said. 'I'm not going to be intimidated by those crooks.' It was said with conviction. 'Dad contacted me from class and suggested it was the right time to actually spill everything I know. Between us we rang people who rang people.'

'This is Megan Phillips,' Harry told them. 'She works in the council offices and has some interesting information.'

'You must be Terry's daughter. He said you'd heard rumours. I'm Anna, from the Italian class.' She leaned across the desk to shake her hand.

'Hi. Yes. Heard a bit more than I was supposed to at the office and I told Dad, but I didn't want to name names and get it wrong. When Dad told me he thought he knew anyway, I realised I had to come forward. I didn't want the wrong people getting into trouble.'

'And there are at least two councillors and two people from the planning office willing to tell their stories, too,' Harry said. 'Seems that various members of the council have been offered bribes. Others have been threatened with the sack if they don't keep quiet.'

'Like me,' Megan said. 'That was the other thing that persuaded me enough was enough. Councillor Stacey's one of the main culprits.'

Stuart nodded.

'Which is what we thought.'

'But who's behind it?' Dante asked.

'I think all may soon be revealed,' Harry said.

'Can we stop playing these games? It's confused matters as it is, innocent

people blaming other innocent people.'
Dante glanced at Stuart who gave him a
rueful smile.

The door opened and in stepped Ross
Harper.

'Good heavens!' he exclaimed as he
peered out of the window at the crowd.
'What the Dickens is this all about, Fellows?'

'We were hoping you could tell us.'
Harry pointed at Ross.

'Surely the Community Centre
rumours have been put to rest.'

'Not that I'm aware of,' Dante said.
'Maybe you'd like to tell us what brings
you here?'

'Harry rang me, as I imagine he did
you.'

'Looks like we're going to have quite
a party,' Rachel said, as the noise of the
crowd grew and dimmed once more.

In the doorway stood a man and
woman in late middle age. Anna recognised the woman immediately as Emily
Buonarotti.

Her guess as to the man's identity was

confirmed when Stuart spoke.

'Dad, thanks for coming.'

Ross hurried across the room.

'Emily. How lovely to see you.'

'Hello, Ross,' was all she replied, her face deadpan.

Ross nodded once at the man beside her.

'Kevin.'

'Ross.'

No smile at all was shared between the two men.

Stuart joined his father.

'Dad, I think there's something you wanted to tell Mrs Buonarotti?'

'Yes, and I'm heartily sorry for it, Emily.'

She looked alarmed.

'For what, exactly, Kevin? Apart from offering me a paltry sum for the business all those years back.'

'Only because I was threatened with having my name blackened. I wouldn't have got any other work if that had happened. I wasn't the one putting up the money for your business, and it certainly wouldn't have belonged to me.

'But I believe the person responsible would have simply claimed he bought it off me. He didn't want to be implicated.' His gaze fell on Ross Harper.

Emily walked forward and stood in front of Ross, her arms crossed as she glared at him.

'And there was you professing your undying love for me. Thank goodness I never got involved with you. What did you think, you'd reduce me to poverty and pick up the pieces?'

'But I offered you work, Emily, when you were struggling. And later, Dante.'

'Only because your original scam didn't pay off. But there was always something about you I didn't like, Ross. You were constantly there, checking up on me. I was convinced at one point you were having me followed. It frightened me, even though I was grateful you put work our way.'

This was getting stranger and stranger, Anna thought. But she was glad that all grounds for Dante and Stuart to be enemies had been removed. What a shame they'd taken so many years to find out the real cause of the problem.

Harry Fellows coughed politely.

'As illuminating as this is, if we could return to the matter in hand.' When he had everyone's attention he continued. 'Now, Megan, if you'd like to reveal the identity of the person putting up the money to bribe the councillors.'

'Councillor Stacey, surely,' Ross said.

'He's certainly up to his neck in it, but he's one of those taking the bribes.'

'Well, this is who I heard it was, anyway, not once, but three times.' Megan frowned, looking nervous. 'I only told Dad this evening when I rang him. Should have said before, really. Do I have to do it here and now, though?' She examined the floor.

'Is this going to take much longer . . . ' Ross said. 'I have to be somewhere else. In fact, I'd better get going. Dante, you can tell me the answer tomorrow.'

Dante shifted his feet and crossed his arms. His mouth was set firm.

'A few more seconds, and I have a feeling we'll all be better informed.'

At that moment there was a crash as the front door was banged against the wall.

'What the . . . ' Harry yelled.

Anna recognised Councillor Stacey from local election photographs. He was huffing and panting, his face crimson.

'The coven has gathered then, has it?' he said. 'Jury and executioners. We'll see who's for the chop, by jingo we will.'

'Megan?' Harry persisted.

She looked even less sure, her fingers clasped together as she looked up from under her eyelashes.

'It's what your dad would want you to do,' Anna told her. She was pretty sure now who she'd name.

'It was him.' Megan pointed straight ahead. 'Ross Harper.'

'I'd like to see anyone prove it.' There was no hint of surprise in Ross's expression. If anything, he looked rather smug.

'Oh, there's several of us who'll confirm it.' Councillor Stacey gave one firm nod of his head.

'Not that it gets you off the hook,' Dante said. 'You're up to your neck in it. As for you, Ross . . . '

'It's a shame, Dan. There could have been a lot of money in it for you, as chief engineer.'

'I wouldn't have touched it with a very large barge pole, pulling down a wonderful Victorian building that should have been listed a long time ago. The next thing I'm going to do is campaign for it.'

'Huh!' Ross said loudly. 'It would have been the most impressive shopping mall in the county. And I would have made a nice contribution towards the council for local benefit, too. It happens all over the country.'

'Councils doing deals with the devil,' Dante said.

'Call it what you like, it's business.'

'The shops you'd have built wouldn't have had affordable rents for the shopkeepers here. It would have killed the local community. As for the nice contribution for local benefit. I've seen it all before — trivial.' Dante spat out the last word.

'Have it your way. I'm off. Good luck with pinning the blame on me without much evidence. And I might win through yet.'

'Not now there's all this fuss,' Councillor Stacey said. 'There's an election next year. None of us would risk it.'

Ross walked to the door, opening it to jeers from the crowd. Terry must have been spreading the word round.

Anna couldn't believe they were allowing him to leave.

'Are we just going to let him go? Can't we call the police or something?'

'I'll be handing over all I know to the police when I leave here,' Harry said. 'Megan's agreed to come with me. I think there'll be a few cases of corruption in public office, among other things.'

'And whatever else happens, Ross has ruined the reputation of his firm,' Dante said. 'That will cost him dearly. As for the others, I'm sure there'll be a few members of the council losing their positions soon, one way or another.' He gave Councillor Stacey a look.

'Tomorrow is another day,' he said, about to exit the office. He faltered, seeing the crowd getting wind of it through the glass door.

'You'll have to go sooner or later,' Harry said. 'I'm not staying here all night.'

The councillor gave them all one more disapproving look before opening the door and bolting for it. The heckling followed him down the road as he scuttled away.

Kevin Keen turned to Emily.

'Do you need a lift back?'

She considered his offer for a short while. 'Yes, that's kind of you. I came by taxi as I thought it would be quicker than parking.'

They took their leave of the others, Stuart calling, 'And thanks for coming down straight away, Dad.'

'Time for us all to go.' Harry picked up a folder and rattled his keys.

'Hurrah for that,' Rachel said, flouncing

to the door. 'I've just about had my fill of this.' Rachel left them, not looking back.

'Charming as ever,' Anna said. 'How on earth do you put up with her all day?'

'She's not too bad in the office,' Dante said. 'And she is a good PA, do anything for me.'

'I bet!'

Dante coloured a little. It enchanted Anna that he was capable of being embarrassed.

'I didn't mean that and you know it. Not my type at all. I'm hoping she'll give the Italian class a wide berth from now on.'

'Hear hear to that! You are going to continue with Italian then?'

'Depends on that lot out there, I guess.' He pointed to Terry's mob, still chanting with enthusiasm.

They all stepped outside. Megan ran over to her father.

'Time for a quick escape,' Dante said. 'Stuart, I'll give you a lift back.'

'No need, it's not far. But there is something you can do for me.'

'Go on.'

'Come and have a drink with me one evening. I'd like to get this misunderstanding completely cleared up and out of the way. It's a shame our friendship was a casualty of it.'

Dante smiled.

'Of course. Time to clear the air.' He took Stuart's offered hand and they shook.

Stuart left them with a spring in his step.

'Dante, Dante, over here!' another voice called. Terry.

Dante stood his ground, looking unsure.

'Do I need this right now?'

'I'll leave you to it.' Harry saluted them and departed.

Anna took his arm, pulling him towards the Italian group.

'Come on, they're smiling at you. I've got a feeling they have something to say.' Dante let her lead him towards them.

★ ★ ★

As they got back into his car, Dante, now in the driver's seat, looked over at Anna, watching her put the seatbelt on.

'What?' she said, not sure she liked being regarded in that way.

'You're the one who seems a bit shaky now.'

She shrugged.

'I'm all right. Just been rather a lot to take in.'

'There's a great sunset tonight. How about we take a walk by the beach? Don't know about you, but I could do with winding down.'

Joy leaped in the pit of her stomach. Being in his company was what she wanted most at this moment.

'Good idea.'

They didn't need to go far, parking on the coast road before heading over the promenade and onto the beach. The tide was three-quarters out. Crunching their way down to where the pebbles met the sand, they took up position next to each other, turning to stroll towards the sunset.

The sky to the west was a lilac-blue blanket, merging into orange as it neared the horizon. The old, burned-out pier stood out in relief against it.

Both of them seemed mesmerised by the marvel of nature in front of them. Anna wanted to speak, but didn't know where to start. A great deal had happened since they'd met again only two months before. And there were other things she longed to tell him, which she knew she was unlikely to.

In the end, he spoke first.

'How is your father getting on now, Anna?'

'Well on the road to recovery.'

'I'm glad to hear that. I know what I'd feel like if something happened to my mother.'

And what about his father? She could understand his resentment towards him, but the fact he went to see him in Rome spoke volumes.

'I guess losing any parent is a shock,' he said, and she wondered if he was referring to her mother or his father, or maybe both. 'My father's staying with a cousin nearby. I've been thinking.' He hunkered down, picking up a scallop shell. 'You used to collect these and paint them.' He handed it to her. She was deeply touched he'd remembered such an insignificant detail.

'I did.' She put it in her pocket. She had none of those painted shells left, but she'd keep this to put in her cloakroom with the other sea memorabilia.

'I still have that one you painted for me, you know,' Dante said. 'Bob Marley.'

'No way!'

'I certainly do. It was amazing. I reckon you could have been an artist.'

'I don't know about that.' She hunkered down to pick up a piece of green sea glass, though it was merely to hide her red face.

'Even Maggie dusts it with great reverence. She's a bit of a Marley fan herself.'

'Maggie?' She stood up, wondering what he was going to reveal next.

'My cleaner.'

'Oh good grief, you don't have a

housekeeper as well, do you?'

'As well as what?'

'As well as who, actually. In this case, Stuart. She also cooks all his meals.'

'Keen has a cook?' He tutted. 'I'll rib him about that when I see him.' Dante chuckled. 'No, I like to cook for myself.'

Anna liked the sound of that.

'To be honest . . .' he said, looking embarrassed, 'I have to have a cleaner because I'm terribly untidy. I can manage tidiness at work, but home is a different story.'

'This Maggie. Does she call you Mr Buonarotti?'

'What? Of course not. Why'd you ask?'

'No reason.'

They started off again, walking more slowly now but soon Dante came to a halt.

'Do you think I should give my father the benefit of the doubt? He says he wants to clean up his act, lay off the booze, make a new start. He was a half decent engineer in his time. I could, well, I could give him a job, something easy to begin with. I don't suppose we'll ever be close, but I could give him a — chance.'

She heard his voice catch. She felt her throat fill up with emotion in response. Despite his harsh treatment of his father, there was a need here to make amends. Or maybe the harsh treatment had been a protection from caring too much.

'I think that's a good idea. What does your mother think?'

'I haven't told her yet. She's semi-retired and wouldn't have to come into too much contact with him. I think it would be OK.'

'Then go with your gut instinct.'

'Thank you. That's helpful.'

She wasn't sure why it had been, but it pleased her that he thought so.

'Do you think . . . ' he began again, halting once again with a sigh. 'Do you think you might ever give me a second chance? I can't tell you how much I regret my decision all those years ago. Stupid, really, to be that secretive. If only I'd confided in you, maybe we could have . . . '

'Shh,' she said, interrupting.

'I'm sorry. Of course it's too late.'

'No, I mean, you don't need to go on explaining, Dante. I've already forgiven you.'

'Have you?'

'Weeks ago.'

They both shifted to face each other. The rich light bathing his features gave him the appearance of a divine statue, like those they'd seen in Rome. She recalled Caroline singing, 'That's Amore'.

'Then, do you think we might . . . ' he started.

'Yes.'

'You don't know what I'm going to say.'

'Yes, I do.'

'Do you know what I'm going to do next then?' He tilted his face, treating her to that lop sided grin that, as a teenager, had always made her fall in love with him anew.

'I've got a pretty good idea.'

'And you don't mind?'

'I just wish you'd jolly well get on with it.'

Anna laughed.

Dante laughed, too, stepping forward to draw her into a close embrace before their lips finally met.